CW01021714

LEVON'S NIGHT

A VIGILANTE JUSTICE THRILLER
BOOK 2

CHUCK DIXON

ROUGH
EDGES
PRESS

LEVON'S NIGHT

1

"It is very bad, sir."

The cop was young and snapped to attention in a rigid salute. Pressed fatigues and body armor. Cap pulled low over his eyes. The one spot of color on his dark uniform was a patch depicting a police officer standing protectively by a pair of children. The lines around the young man's mouth were deep. His voice husky with emotion.

"I have seen bad," Ramon Salas said, stepping into the shade of the awnings over the broad veranda. The day was already hot, the sun up only a few hours. The breeze off the Caribbean was doing little more than stirring the muggy air along the Costa Rican coast.

"Very bad, sir," the young cop repeated and led the way through the expansive villa toward the main crime scene at the back. There were secondary crime scenes outside the big house. Two bodies lay outside; Ramon saw them from the back of the police cruiser on his way in. One by the wrought iron access gate. Another on the circular turn-around before the main entrance. Both bodies appeared to be men covered in sheets. Flower print sheets taken from the house to preserve the dignity of the dead. The forensics team from *Departamento de Medicina Legal* would scold the answering cops for tampering with evidence. The cops from the *Fuerza Publica* stood about the bodies like ants around crumbs of bread. Black uniforms and body armor. They smoked and talked while waiting for someone like Ramon to show up. Someone who would take the bloody mess off their hands.

The house sat on a hill overlooking the sea. All spread out with outbuildings that formed a courtyard around an enormous saltwater pool. Ten thousand square feet maybe. On a ten-acre parcel in Puntayamas. Many millions in American dollars. The interior was cool with stale air-conditioned air. The rooms went on and on toward the back of the house.

Ramon walked past walls lined with paintings. He knew nothing of paintings. The walls of his home displayed pictures of his children. To him, the paintings in their expensive frames looked like something his kids might have done. When they were four. And drunk.

The eager young cop stood aside and gestured with an open hand into a wide arched opening. He reminded Ramon of a presenter on a Mexican game show. *And here are your prizes, señor.*

The room had a high ceiling two stories in height. It was a large area meant for entertaining. Lots of uphol-stered conversation pits comprised of long sofas uphol-stered in cool linen and layered with mountains of embroidered throw pillows. A projection system for a TV screen that dominated a 100-foot wall. The wall facing the back of the house was glass from end to end and ceiling to floor. The ocean filled the eyes. The morning sun turned the water to silvery shimmers. The remaining face of the room was dominated by a long bar with a full kitchen behind it. Shelves stocked with bottles. Behind the glass doors of a stand-up cooler Ramon could see row after row of bottled beer. Imported brands in green bottles. He licked his lips despite the earliness of the hour.

In an open area before the bar was the main crime scene. Three adult figures sat in steel framed chairs. Patio chairs dragged in off the veranda for this purpose. They were draped in sheets like the bodies out front. Ramon could see the exposed arm of a woman. She was secured to the arms of the chair with black tape at her wrists and elbows. Broad bands of tape held her ankles secured to the metal legs. More tape below the knee. Whoever did this was practiced.

The three adults sat in a row next to one another like members of an audience.

Or witnesses.

Across from them sat two more figures, smaller figures. Similarly bound with black tape. They looked tiny beneath the sheets that covered them like tents. A tasteful monochromatic print of palm fronds. Beneath the chairs was a joined pool of dried blood shining black in the sunlight slanting in through the window wall. In the sticky spill Ramon could see pale objects.

Fingers. The fingers of children.

One had a flower, a daisy, meticulously painted on the nail.

The eager young policeman was right.

This one was bad.

2

They told him that being bilingual would be a plus.

Fluency in Spanish and English would lead to advancement in the Bureau, everyone said.

Instead, it led to shit assignments like the one Bill Marquez was being briefed on now.

"Got a liaise job down in Costa Rica for you. Should be cake since you're Mexican."

"I'm Dominican, sir," Bill said.

ADC Terry Blount squinted at Bill from across his desk. Sunlight filtered by LA smog glared through the window. The sounds of traffic from down on Wilshire filled the silence.

"That's not a problem, is it?" Blount said.

"Da nada." Bill smiled and shrugged.

ADC Blount let out a sigh. The FBI had become totally politicized in recent years. Every utterance had to be checked before it was spoken in order not to offend. A special agent used the word "siesta" in a surveillance report three years ago. The shitstorm of paperwork, hearings and mandatory seminars handed down from Justice went on for six months. The last thing the assistant director in charge needed was another weekend spent at a sensitivity course for thinking every beaner in his office was a Mexican.

"Okay. We're good. Thanks for being cool about that, Bill." Blount used his first name. We're all buds here, right? Amigos.

"A liaison job, sir?" Bill said.

"Remember Corey Blanco?"

"The Ponzi guy? Took a bunch of investors for a ride. Mall real estate, right?"

"And an escrow surety company he bought then picked the clients' accounts clean. Got away with almost a half billion," Blount said.

"Got away is right. I'm guessing the trail got hot again?" Bill sat forward. They were sending him after one of Justice's most wanted felons?

"Hot then cold. Corey Blanco is dead. Homicide down in Costa Rica. Whole family. The OIJ in CR is investigating. When they found out who they had they called State who called the AG who called us looking for someone to send down."

"So, no investigation, sir?"

"No. You're going down there at the request of State and the Costa Rican government. Dot the *I's* and cross the *T's*. Take an extra day and wiggle your toes in the sand."

"Thank you, sir. But won't there be evidence down there?"

"Evidence, Marquez?" They were back to last names.

"The funds Blanco got away with were never recovered. Hundreds of millions were taken from innocent investors. There might be something down there on a hard drive or paper. We might find some of those funds."

"Tell you what. If you find any bank receipts lying around with lots of zeroes on them, you give me a call.

We'll send a team down. Otherwise, you are there to bear witness, sign forms and confirm the identity of the deceased. You *comprende* that?"

"*Si,*" Bill said, biting the inside of his mouth to keep the sarcasm from escaping.

"So, email or paper?" ADC Blount said, fingers poised over his keyboard.

"Email. I'll read it on the plane, sir."

"Your flight's at four. LAX. Get your toothbrush and jammies and get over there."

3

"It was very bad," Captain Ramon Salas of the *Organismo de Investigación Judicial* shouted, bending under the prop wash of the Huey they'd sent to ferry Bill to the crime scene.

"Okay," was all Bill could say in answer to that as he took the older man's offered hand.

They made introductions as they crossed the flagstone parking area where the chopper set down and toward the sprawling villa of the late, ex-patriate fugitive felon Corey Blanco. The two men were from roughly equivalent agencies, investigating crimes that rose above a certain bar of malfeasance, national security, or broad federal guidelines of misbehavior. Salas was much more senior. It wasn't just the gray in his dark hair. It was the lines around the eyes and mouth. The face of a cop a few decades on the job. Bill liked him immediately.

Captain Salas led him through the house, past the few uniformed cops that had been left behind to keep lookie-loos and looters away. Surfaces of furniture, walls, light switches, and doors showed the greasy residue of a thorough fingerprint search. The carpets were trampled flat by the passage of many feet. Paintings on the wall were askew. *Was that a Matisse study?* Furniture had been moved aside to allow passage for cops, forensics, investigators, and coroners.

The big room at the back of the house had yellow tape strung across one end cutting the room in half. LA LINEA DE LA POLICIA NO CRUZADO. One side was a dream home theater area — the other something out of a nightmare.

Three chairs sat across from two more. There was blood sprayed over the scene with a large stain beneath the pair of chairs facing into the room. Carefully cut strips of black duct tape were still stuck to the legs and arms. The set-up was obvious. The three chairs facing the water were for spectators. The two seats with their backs to the sea were the main show.

"Tell me what happened," Bill said, touching fingers to a strip of yellow barrier tape. He'd get some answers before he set foot in the crime scene.

"Señor Blanco, his wife and their housekeeper were seated in the row of three chairs. The Blanco's two children, a boy of six and a girl of ten, were seated there," Salas said and gestured to the chairs in the pool of blood.

"Causes of death?"

"The children, in the end, had their throats cut. Señora Blanco and the housekeeper were each smothered with plastic bags cinched over their heads."

"And Corey Blanco?"

"Heart attack."

"What was that?" Bill said, turning to Captain Salas.

"Señor Blanco suffered a massive coronary. There were no wounds to his body," Salas said.

Bill stood for a moment, looking at the scene of horror that marred this beautiful home.

"How did the killers gain entry?"

"From the sea. Or they came along the beach from another point. All evidence was erased by the tide. So it is merely a guess. The front gates are covered by cameras. There are other cameras along the road leading to this house. Many families of wealth live on this beach. Security is complete. No unrecognized cars used the road the night of the murders."

"There was private security?" Bill asked. The kitchen and bar were untouched. The killers did not help themselves to booze or snacks — all business.

"Two men listed as assistants to Señor Blanco. One was found dead at the front gate. Another on the drive before the house."

"Cause of death?"

"Blunt force trauma of some kind. We're not certain of the weapon. They were each taken from behind by blows to the head powerful enough to fracture their skulls."

"Unusual." Bill made a note to look into the bodyguards' backgrounds.

"We thought so as well," Salas agreed.

"Anything else?" Bill asked.

"Follow me," Salas said and turned to walk away. Bill followed.

In the home gym they arrived at a wall safe, a vault really, hidden behind a door disguised as just another mirrored panel in a long, mirrored wall. The vault was six feet tall with shelves and drawers within. The contents were spilled on the floor. Bearer bonds. Some bundles of cash. Jewelry. Passports.

"It is all untouched. We wanted to leave this as we found it until your people arrived," Salas said and met Bill's eyes with a level gaze.

The message was clear. *We took nothing. We are not thieves.*

"This safe wasn't forced open. Someone opened it for them. Probably under duress," Bill said and crouched to look at the valuable litter lying in a heap between an elliptical machine and a stationary bike. He took a pen from his jacket pocket and used it to poke through the pile.

"We surmised it was Señor Blanco. They brought him here and he opened the safe for them," Salas said.

"Almost a million in Yankee dollars here. About the same in Euros. And God knows how much in bonds and jewelry. I'd say they didn't find what they were looking for."

"Why not take what is lying here for the taking? Most of it is untraceable, no?"

"Because whatever they were looking for makes even what's on the floor here look like chump change," Bill said and flipped open a passport with the pen tip. Mrs. Blanco was young and pretty. Pretty enough to take a good passport photo.

"*Que?* Chump change?" Salas said, peering over Bill's shoulder at the open passport.

"*Poco poco.*"

"I see. Chump change."

"Blanco opened the safe for them. What they wanted wasn't here. So they tortured his kids to make him talk. He had a heart attack and spoiled their plans. Stress, probably."

"But he let these men torture his children for a very long time," Salas said, recalling the autopsy report.

"Maybe that's the kind of hard man Blanco was. Or maybe seeing what they were doing tripped his heart off. Maybe they kept on going hoping the wife knew what they were looking for. I'm betting she didn't. They left here empty-handed."

"Jesus Maria. What were they looking for?" Salas sighed.

Bill Marquez stood and replaced his pen in his jacket pocket.

"Corey Ray Blanco got away with over seven hundred million dollars from investor fraud and outright theft. Subtracting this house and whatever he spent on his wife and kids the past decade still leaves a shitload of cash somewhere. These men were after that. The whole enchilada."

"*Que?*"

"An enchilada is like a burrito, I guess."

Salas laughed at that.

"Yeah. Right. 'The *whole* enchilada' means everything. They want it all."

"And your FBI will send more agents to try and find the men who did this thing? These men will be far away from Costa Rica by now. I do not have the means to pursue this any further."

"I'm going to tell you the truth, Captain," Bill said. "My bureau could give a shit about the men who killed this family. But my government has more than a few agencies who'd like to find Blanco's money. All I have to do is convince them it's worth looking for."

"And you? What do *you* wish to find?" Salas said, studying Bill's eyes.

"I want the animals who could do something like this. And I want them soon. Because I don't think this is the end of all this. I think it's just the start." Bill excused himself to make satellite phone calls to a few numbers back in the States.

Levon Cade sat forward in the upholstered leather chair. His elbows on knees. Neither sitting nor rising but poised for either.

"I wish you'd make yourself comfortable," the thin-faced, bearded man said to him.

"I am comfortable, Doctor," Levon said.

"You can call me by my name. Justin." Dr. Justin Ayres smiled where he sat lounging back in the swivel chair he'd pulled from behind his office desk in order to sit closer to Levon.

Levon scanned the room. An office with a few too many personal touches to be entirely professional. Bookshelves packed with textbooks and file folders in standing plastic cases. There was a Superman action figure next to a framed photo of Dr. Ayres kayaking through white water. A potted plant by the window, fronds stretched to reach through the slats of the partly open blinds. The desk, an antique or heirloom, was stacked with file folders held together with rubber bands. An open laptop occasionally made muted cartoon noises.

They sat that way for a while. Not talking. Levon unmoving yet kinetic. Dr. Ayres smiling easily over templed fingers, eyes on Levon's face.

"You mentioned post-traumatic stress," Dr. Ayres said after a while, giving up, for now, on having his new patient call him by his first name.

"I'm not sleeping. I have dreams," Levon said.

"Nightmares?"

"Memories."

Dr. Ayres nodded.

"It's not me so much that I worry about. It's my little girl. I'm, I guess you'd say, a single father? She worries about me."

"So, these dreams don't cause terrors? Sudden waking?"

"No, Doctor. Nothing like that."

"You've tried medications?"

"Xanax. Zoloft. Ambien. A few others. They make me feel like I have a blanket over my head. There has to be another way."

"You don't like the side effects of the drugs?"

"I'm trying to be good father. That won't happen if I'm gooned up on sedatives all the time. Only, the insomnia and memories don't help either. I feel like I'm pulling away from her. You understand?"

"Yes. I think I do. Have you thought of keeping a journal?"

"Like a diary?" Levon said, looking into the doctor's eyes.

"Diaries are for teenage girls. I mean a record of your thoughts. Maybe if you put these memories of yours on paper, organized them from random thoughts into a narrative. It might help you make more sense of them. Put them into context and, hopefully, put them into the past. What branch of the service were you in?"

"Is that important, Doctor?"

"No, not so much."

"You think writing down my thoughts would help. It might work. And to be honest, I'm all the way up in Hermon. I can't be driving down here to Millinocket every week. It's a two-hour trip. If a journal would help me work things out, then I could just see you now and then."

"Certainly. But we still have twenty minutes to this session so if you wanted—"

Levon rose from the edge of the chair and reached back for his wallet.

"The girl out front handles payments." Dr. Ayres jumped from his seat with a hand up.

Levon took him by the wrist and pressed a wad of cash into his hand.

"No thanks, Doctor. We'll handle this between ourselves," Levon said and showed himself out.

Dr. Ayres reseated himself and piloted his chair back behind his desk where he unfolded the cash. It was four times his usual hourly rate for therapy.

"Cathy!" he called.

Cathy, with a quizzical expression, appeared in his doorway.

"Can you get me the contact details for Joshua Randall?" he said, sweeping the cash into his middle desk drawer.

"Who?" she said, tilting her head.

"My last patient. The man who just left here," Dr. Ayres said, losing patience with his idiot sister-in-law whom his wife had made him hire.

"Was that his name? He handed the contact forms back without filling them in," she said and turned to go back to the solitaire game she was playing at the reception desk.

The evergreen trees loomed close on either side of the road, stretching up to join the night sky above to form a tunnel of dark around them. The twin beams of the Dodge Ram's headlights stabbed ahead with no answering lights coming from the other direction as far as the eyes could see. The two-lane cut across the county as straight as a string through mile after mile of uninterrupted pine forest.

"Smells like snow," Merry said from where she was buckled in on the passenger side.

"Since when can an Alabama girl smell snow?" Levon said at the wheel.

"I'm a Maine girl now. A Maniac," she said and smiled.

"Not with that accent."

"What accent?"

"That biscuits and gravy drawl of yours, little honey child," he said, laying more syrup on his voice for effect.

"You sound like a Squidbilly!" she said laughing.

He had no idea what that was.

"You find everything on your list?" he said.

"Sure did. Everything go okay at the dentist? I forgot to ask," she said.

"No cavities," he lied. No need to tell her he saw a therapist. He'd left her for the hour at a place that served breakfast all day. Her favorite meal. She deserved a little spoiling, and waffles and berries with cream was what she wanted. She'd been working on a placemat puzzle when he got back. It was slow in the afternoon with the leaf peepers long gone and winter closing in. A waitress sat in the booth working the puzzle with her. Levon left an eye-popping tip before father and daughter departed to do some shopping.

They'd driven down I-95 to Bangor, the first time they'd seen anything like a real city since moving up to Lake Bellevue. Levon lied to the doctor about living in Hermon, just as he'd lied about almost every other detail of his life other than having a daughter and living with a mind filled with ugly memories.

Outside Bangor they explored a big box outdoor mall and loaded up the Ram with groceries and necessaries for the long winter ahead. They bought cases of canned goods and frozen vegetables and fruit. Cases of juice and powdered milk. As many cartons of eggs as they thought would keep. Splurged on some frozen pizzas and ice cream tubs. Big family packs of chicken, beef, fish, and a Virginia cured ham for Christmas day. Bags of fresh potatoes, carrots, and onions. All paid for in cash. It would stay cold in the back of the Ram with the thermometer at thirty and heading down.

They agreed to separate for thirty minutes to buy surprises for each other for Christmas. They met in front of an office supply store the size of a hangar for a jumbo jet. Merry had a bag under her arm from Barnes & Noble. Levon had already slipped back to the truck to hide his package. The telltale shape would give away the surprise. He'd also made a quick trip into the office supply store to pick up a Moleskine journal and bag of pens.

They stopped at a Wendy's for dinner before setting out on the long ride back home to Bellevue. They picked up some extra burgers and fries to take along. With winter coming on it would be a long time before they saw fast food again. Even reheated it would be a treat for Merry. Then back north on 95 for their new home.

"You sorry we moved way out in the back of beyond, honey?" Levon asked. He flipped on the high beams. This road was notorious for collisions with deer and even black bears.

"Nope. Those teachers were asking a lot of questions," she said, leaning forward to twiddle the dial on the radio to find a fresh station as they drove out of range of the one she'd been listening to.

"So homeschooling is okay with you?"

"Well, my teacher sometimes falls asleep in class," she said with a sly glance his way.

"Sorry, honey."

It was true. His nights were snatches of sleep interrupted by his own racing thoughts. But a half dozen math flashcards and he was out like a light. It was a good thing that Merry was an eager learner and a self-starter. She got that from her mother. He monitored her tests and organized the curriculum he'd bought at a Learning Center in Bangor. But she did all the reading on her own and was moving through fifth grade at a steady clip. And the teachers at the school she'd attended under the name Mary Tallmadge *were* a nosy bunch. They wouldn't let up on their personal lives and what the Tallmadges were like at home. Merry had to spend as much time inventing answers for them as she did on her homework. The stress was showing on her to a degree that even Levon, as preoccupied as he was, noticed.

She was excited when her father came up with the idea of them packing up and taking off farther north to a resort community where they could be anonymous tourists all summer and reclusive locals during the cold months when the population fell to include only those hardy natives willing to face the brutal weather and utter isolation. He was Mitch Roeder now and she was Moira Roeder. They'd lost his wife and her mother to cancer a few years back. That part was true and no one they met was tactless enough to ask questions about that. And any reply they made to questions would be heartfelt and honest because they were mostly the truth. This was upstate Maine. People might wonder but they'd never ask. And mostly, they never even bothered to wonder why a dad and daughter with Dixie accents picked the desolate center of Maine to call home. People came to this state to get away from their problems, not to be pestered about them.

"You sure you don't miss having friends?" he asked.

"I didn't really make any back at Lewiston. 'Sides, there's kids at the lake in the summer, right? And Carl and Giselle live nearby. They're pretty cool," she said, sitting back in place after locating a fuzzy Radio Disney channel on the radio.

"What makes them cool?"

"Well, Carl has all those comic books and he lets me read them. And Giselle's a couple years older than me but she promised to teach me to ski cross-country."

"I guess they're pretty cool then," he said.

She leaned forward and turned her head to look up at the lowering sky.

"Now it *looks* like snow," she said.

And it did. The sky above was dense from horizon to

horizon with thick cloud cover bringing an early dusk. There was a tang to the air as the barometer fell.

Merry was asleep in her seat and breathing gently when the first flakes fell hours later. He reached forward to snap off the hiss of the radio; the last stations had been left miles and miles behind. Levon listened to the wipers move before him and watched the swirling flakes gray in his high beams piercing the black between the ranks of pines down the lonely forest road that was taking them home.

6

Bill Marquez was all innocence and "golly-gee!" when ADC Blount informed him that the IRS had taken an interest in the Corey Blanco murder.

What Bill didn't tell his boss was that he'd back-doored this one by telling a friend at Treasury what he found down in Costa Rica. Word got around about a team of professional criminals with a line on the stolen Blanco fortune and six kinds of hell erupted all over DC. A task force was formed, and Treasury sent some marshals down to San Carlos. Not to miss his own party, Blount sent Bill back down with some Bureau forensics guys to help out and share in any good news. It was still a Treasury case so there'd be no blowback to the LA office if they came up with nothing to show for the trip except new tans.

Truth was, federal agents weren't really detectives. Certainly not homicide. And Bureau agents were barely cops. More like lawyers with guns. But there were a few former city cops among the T-men and two of them had worked in big city homicide divisions. Tony Marcoon in Philly and Ben Greco in Chicago. After a few days of work around the Blanco villa the two collated what they'd found and told the story.

"The actors came in by sea. We have a shit-ton of witnesses north and south and no one saw anyone strange on their private beaches that night," Ben Greco started. He had a PowerPoint set up in a vacant house they were borrowing with the permission of the absent owner and the local Costa Rican law who were sitting in. The group was seated in a media room using the big screen for the presentation. On the screen were the images on Greco's laptop with windows for a layout of the home, map of the coast and pictures of the crime scene.

Tony Marcoon stepped in, prompted by notes in an open book before him.

"One neighbor was having a party on the adjoining beach to the north. An all-nighter. Lots of potential witnesses. Nobody saw anything. To the south we have a paranoid dude with credentials almost as shaky as Blanco's. He has motion lights on his house that are set to light up if anything bigger than a dog passes by. No lights that night. And he has cameras that caught nothing but surf and seagulls."

"They came in off the ocean. By boat or raft or what?" Bill asked. He was seated by Captain Salas who was trying to hide his enthusiasm at being included in the fast-moving briefing. His English was strictly grammar school and Bill was providing translations *sotto voce* as things went on.

"They could have used a fucking submarine. The local coast guard are doing what they can, but you have to understand there's a lot of pleasure craft in these waters. These guys could have hopped on a Zodiac off a yacht or fishing boat and come ashore and no one would have seen or heard a thing," Ben Greco answered.

"The actors gained entry to the property. We have no clear count on how many we're talking about here. They either took care of the two guards first and then entered the house, or there could even have been enough of them to split up and perform the two tasks simultaneously," Tony said.

"The alarms were bypassed but they may not even have been on. Estimated time of death on the guards, and they were the first to die, is early evening. Just as it was getting dark. So the house probably wasn't buttoned down for the night. Time of death for the others was several hours later, estimated. Four hours inside. Seven hours outside," Ben said paraphrasing his notes.

Up on the screen was a slideshow of photographs taken by Salas's team. Corey Blanco with his head slumped forward as though he'd merely dozed off in his chair. His wife was limp in her chair against the duct tape restraints. Her mane of blond hair hid her face inside the tight confines of the plastic bag secured over her head. The house maid's face was mottled black with broken blood vessels, and her swollen tongue protruded against the suffocating plastic like a snail looking to escape. As bad as they were, it was the photos of the children that made even the most hardened agents turn their heads away. One of them, a T-man (woman actually) whose days were spent examining counterfeit currency for flaws and patterns, rushed from the room to get noisily sick in another room. One tough US Marshal motherfucker had tears on his face as he forced himself to look at the garishly lit photos projected on the state-of-the-art big screen.

"Yeah," Tony said. "These are sick fuckers we're looking for. But they're pros. This was a professional start to finish. Ex-military or established gang. A tight crew that doesn't take naps in the getaway car or brag to strangers in a bar about scores. No DNA. No prints. None of these guys took a dump or a piss while they were in there."

"Make no mistake. We *want* these guys. We want their *asses.* Our masters in DC and Quantico may have a stiff prick for the Blanco cash but it's *these* assholes we want. They are the key to finding the cash. Find them, *any* of them, book them and press them, and we'll find the money," Ben put in. Iron and fire in his words. He had kids of his own from two marriages. The man was outraged.

"That's just it, guys. Did they get the money?" Bill Marquez said, holding one hand over the other on his lap to keep from raising it like a second grader in math class.

"What's that mean?" Ben said without rancor.

"I don't think they got jack shit. I think they walked out of here with blue balls is what I mean. Put the house diagram up again," Bill said, standing. Tony tapped keys. Bill walked up to the screen and began pointing to spots on the house layout that reappeared, much to everyone's relief, in place of the murder photos.

Bill said, "They had Blanco open the safe for them. I think he did it first thing. Maybe thinking this was just a home invasion. But what they wanted isn't in the safe. What they wanted is the big bundle. So they take Blanco back to the big room where his family and the house-keeper are already strapped down. They make threats, then they start to make good on the threats."

"On the kids. So does Blanco still hold out a while?" Tony Marcoon asked.

"We'll never know. The man was hard-hearted enough of a son-of-a-bitch to take the life savings away from old people and families. But you have to think that was all business. They start on his own children and maybe he wants to fold, wants to give them anything to make it stop. In any case, I think his heart gave out before he could give them anything."

"Then the *señora*," Ramon Salas spoke up from his seat.

"Yeah. I shared some of this with the captain before. They keep working on the kids hoping that the mother knows what they want. She doesn't. It's hours of this but she has nothing to give them. They finally kill the remaining four and then leave, going back out to sea the way they came. Empty handed." Bill showed his audience the palms of his hands.

"That's fucked up. For us and for them. There's no angle for us. If they got something, then we could be on the lookout for large sums of cash being moved. If what you're saying is what happened, then there's no handle," Ben Greco said with disgust.

"Maybe they didn't get Blanco's secret," Bill said. "That doesn't mean Blanco didn't leave something somewhere. Just not here in the Costa Rica house. Maybe not the hard cash but a way *to* the cash. This house is loaded with leads if we know where to look. If we find what they were looking for, we can get to it before them. We can be waiting for them."

"He's right," the female agent with the twitchy stomach said, returning to the room, a damp washcloth held against the back of her neck.

"Nancy Vargas. Special agent, Treasury," Ben Greco said by way of introduction.

"I work forensic accounting. This murder shit is too real for me. But what we have here is numbers and paper trails. Corey Blanco dropped off the grid a decade ago. We've never been able to pick up a thread on him. But this house is a start. Even paying with cash there's legalities to consider. He had to use a name and that name ties to other names and other places. It's the first square on the board. We just need to find the rest of the squares and figure out what the board looks like." She took a cautious sip of ginger ale from the glass by her seat.

"I sucked at math," Tony Marcoon said, grinning.

"Blanco might have other properties. We need to find out if he moved around at all, and where he went and who he had contact with. We don't know what the assholes we're looking for know now. Maybe they learned something, the location of the next square," Nancy said.

"You think he has other houses somewhere? You think the money's there?" Bill said.

"I think he left himself options. Back doors. Escape contingencies. Blanco was smart. He got away with it, and he knew he'd have to hide the rest of his life. He'd have planned for that," she said.

"Find his hiding place ahead of these fucks and we'll be waiting for them when they stick their hand in," Ben Greco said.

"There's something else to think about," Nancy Vargas said.

"Tell us, teacher," Tony Marcoon said.

"The money might be squirreled away in banks. The quiet kind of banks. What we're looking for might be account numbers and Swift codes. A list," she said.

"A single piece of paper that could be anywhere in the world," Bill said.

"Yeah," she said and took another tentative swig of Canada Dry.

———

First Entry
12/23

Wasted half the morning sitting here thinking of something to write.

Guess I should write about that.

Writing my thoughts down is hard. Trust is hard. Even though no one will see these words but me.

Maybe that means I don't trust myself.

That's about all the deep thoughts I can handle for one day.

Two days till Xmas. M is bouncing off the walls.

Hope she likes the skis.

7

Levon pulled the Ram up to the single gas pump in front of the Bellevue Market and Hardware. The lot was plowed and shoveled around the pump island. Three feet of snow since Thanksgiving. The county road was lined with high berms shoved aside by the plows.

A Range Rover was parked on the opposite side of the island. A man stood with hands in the pockets of a woolen coat while the tank filled. The Rover was new but covered over in a patina of salt.

"I will be done in a minute, okay?" The man stood stamping his feet almost in time with the dinging bell on the pump. The pump had one hose. An old Texaco with the flying horse symbol faded pink on the steel hood.

"I need to go inside anyway. I'm Mitch," Levon said putting out a gloved hand.

"Sascha," the man said smiling. Levon couldn't see through the fogged over glasses to see if the smile reached his eyes. He wore corduroy pants and sandals over thick woolen socks.

"Short for Alexander?" Levon said, giving the man's limp hand a single pump.

The man hesitated before nodding.

Levon left him stamping and pumping to cross the gravel lot, avoiding the puddles of slush that gathered in the depressions. The door of the store banged open and a woman stamped toward him, head down. She nearly walked into him on her way to the pump.

"Excuse me," he said.

She looked up, eyes goggling through thick glasses misting with condensation. The bitter expression twisting her face turned into a beaming smile. An explosion of red hair was barely contained by a red and white striped knit tosh.

"I am sorry. That woman, she…" she said, turning her head toward the store with a wince.

"Cecile? Some days I'd rather run into a bear behind the counter. I'm Mitch." Levon nodded and offered his hand.

"Lily. You live on Mohawk Road? With your family?" she said, giving his hand a firm grasp in a wool mitten decorated with reindeer.

"Just my daughter and me. Do you have kids?"

"No. Only Sascha and I. We are artists."

"Painting?"

She squinted at him.

"What kind of art do you do?"

"Oh. Concept art, Graphics. It looks like we are ready to go." She nodded to where Sascha was replacing the nozzle on the hook.

"Well, see you around the lake then. Merry Christmas," he said and watched her pick her way around the slush puddles. She also wore sandals over socks. They were in the Rover and gone across the county road and hooking a left to Mohawk Road without a wave or word of farewell.

"Wanted to know if I had the *New York Times*, if you

can believe that," Cecile said by way of greeting when Levon entered the store, muggy and warm after the bitter cold outside.

"Well, they're artists." Levon shrugged.

"The goddamn *New York Times*," she huffed behind the counter. Cecile was a woman of indeterminate age who gave the impression that the store she stocked and managed simply grew up around her one day. It fit her like a turtle's shell.

A grocery store with two rows of mostly empty shelves in the offseason. A pair of coolers stood against the back wall loaded with sodas, beer, lunchmeats, dairy, cheeses, and bacon. The longest wall held racks of chips and candy bars. A spinner rack of dog-eared paperbacks was the town's unofficial public library. Behind the counter was a wall of cigarettes and cigars. A broad arch at the rear of the grocery opened into a reasonably well-stocked hardware store filled with necessities for emergency repairs and simple DIY jobs. During the summer, the place was hopping with tourists coming north and south on the county road. Cecile had the only gas, smokes, and snacks for thirty miles in either direction, with signs alerting drivers to that spotted all along the shoulder in either direction. In the winter, her customer base was limited to the locals and anyone who was wintering around the lake.

"I told her that after Thanksgiving, even the mail doesn't come every day. I'll be damned if I'll stock a newspaper that I'll never sell anyway. I told her, 'You want to know what's going on in New York you should Google it,'" Cecile continued.

"Artists," was all Levon could bring to the exchange.

"I suppose."

"Did that PVC pipe order come in, Cecile?"

"It did. You can find it in back. The joints are in a box with your name marked on it."

"Great. I'm going to work on the Hoffert kitchen over the holidays," Levon said.

"And where's that darling little girl of yours?" Cecile leaned on the counter, her entire demeanor changed. The wrinkles on her face deepened to allow a toothy smile to open.

"Home with her studies."

"This close to Christmas?"

"She has to finish her language and math sections then she gets to take two weeks," Levon said as he picked up a fistful of Merry's favorite candy bars. Mallow Cups and Snickers.

"Those for her?"

"Stocking stuffers."

"Nothing for Dad?" she said with a conspiratorial wink.

"This," Levon said, holding up a Payday.

"I think Dad deserves something better than that," Cecile said and bent to root around under the counter. She came up with a black cardboard tube embossed with gold and silver letters.

"Glenfiddich eighteen-year-old Scotch. Picked up a case at an estate sale. One fifty," she said.

"One hundred. Cash. When did you get a liquor license?"

"Call the cops. They'll be here in a week maybe. And you always pay cash anyway, Mitch. One twenty."

"Sold. I need something for Nate Fenton anyway. $40 for the pump and whatever I owe for the PVC pipes and candy," Levon said and counted out twenties on the counter.

"Candy's on me. You give my love to your little one," Cecile said and bagged the Scotch for him.

———

Third Entry
12/25

Christmas was good.
M was surprised by the skis.
Will spend the winter reading the two-volume history of
the Civil War she gave me.
More snow on the way.

8

A sound awakened Sefa in the night. A sound that made him think the owners of the house were home.

He turned to the girl lying next to him on the king-sized bed in the master suite. He touched her naked shoulder. Sefa wanted to ask if she heard the sound, too. She was dead to the world, sleeping off the primo hashish they both smoked the night before out on the tennis courts behind the house. Try as he might, he couldn't recall her name. She was Dutch maybe?

Sefa slipped from the bed and pulled a pair of baggy shorts over his skinny ass. If the owners were home, he'd have to get himself and the girl out of here. Even through his hash-addled brain Sefa could recall the many contingencies he'd worked out for just this scenario. If only he could wake up the Swede in his bed. Or was she German?

He'd been living here for over a year, rent-free. Sefa was a Fijian, a local born on the north island of Vanua Levu. The first time he came to this big house at the end of Otu Point was as a worker in a gardening crew contracted to do regular maintenance on the ground for the absentee owners. On his second visit to the house, he simply hid when the crew climbed onto the truck for the trip back to Nadi.

No one missed him.

He never left.

That's how Sefa Buwawa, bastard son of a shrimp fisherman, began life as a millionaire. The owners were far away and, from what he could tell by playing detective, had not been here since their second child was born. It served them right to have an unwanted house guest. Rich Anglo pigs having so much money that they could have a house thousands of times the size of the apartment he and his eight siblings grew up in, and never even come visit. All he had to do was stay in the house when the gardeners came once every two weeks, and all was cool.

There was little food. The wall of freezers and refrigerators in the gourmet kitchen were long empty and shut down. The pantry had some canned goods and he'd lived on those for a few weeks. He put on some clothes from one of the walk-in closets and hitched a ride down to Denarau where the cruise ships came in. He didn't realize that he'd chosen the wife's closet to raid. But the silk pants suit fit him reasonably well and he cut a dashing figure; creamy silk against his dark skin set off by a royal blue blouse. He never noticed it buttoned from the wrong side.

It was ridiculously easy to pick up foreign girls in the hotel bars that lined the streets and embarcaderos. Sefa was a good-looking kid with an easy manner built upon the plain fact that he never had anything to lose and would just throw himself into social situations until he was thrown back out. To everyone who knew him, he was an asshole. But to these European, Japanese, and American bitches, he seemed funny, exotic, and harmless

with his stupid jokes told in halting English. The drugs-
and all the girls had drugs-made him seem even more of
a charmer.

Australian girls were the only ones who never fell for
his bullshit. Stuck up Aussie twats.

He would draw them back to the big house with
stories of his wealthy family who were back home in
India. The girls usually had a rental car or would spring
for a taxi. Sefa was *always* losing his wallet, wouldn't you
know? They were invariably gob smacked by the size of
the house. The girl last night said "*unglaublich*" when she
saw the pool. Was that German or Dutch? Every girl he
brought back easily bought his explanation that the electric was out because of a recent storm and these damned
Fijians they hired to get it back online were just too
fucking lazy to fix it right.

Now his life of playing Fijian millionaire, getting laid
by tourist girls, and getting high was coming to an end as
indicated by the sounds from the other side of the house.

He crept barefoot over the tile and crouched behind a
knee-high wall that ran across a big gallery room sepa-
rating a media area from a music room complete with a
Steinway grand piano. Sefa raised his head over the sill
of the wall just enough to peer over it and through the
opening that led to the home gym.

These weren't the homeowners returning for the
Christmas holidays.

Men in mechanic's coveralls were going around the
gym, breaking the glass off the mirrored walls. He could
see four men from his vantage point. They all wore vinyl
gloves on their hands and cloth booties over their boots.
A fifth man joined them carrying a pair of heavy toolboxes in from outside. Big boxes made of red-painted
metal. One of the mirrored panels fell to shards,
revealing the shining steel door of a safe set in the wall.

Two of the men swept the broken glass away and moved the exercise equipment aside while another pair opened the toolboxes to remove power tools and attachments. The fifth man stood waiting, casually smoking one of those electronic cigarettes.

The smoking man had a bush of dark hair atop his head. The sides were shaved close. He spoke to the others in a mumbled tongue that sounded to Sefa's ear like French but not French. He turned as if to look right at Sefa. One of his eyes was milky white with a heavy lid that fell over it as if half of his face was dozing. One whole side of his face looked frozen as if paralyzed. The effect spoiled what might have been handsome features.

Startled, Sefa dropped back into his crouch and crab-walked back the way he'd come.

A vinyl gloved hand clamped over his mouth. An arm snaked around his neck, cutting off his wind in an instant. His bare feet left the floor with a jerk.

The Fijian millionaire prayed to every god he knew (and he knew a lot of them) to not let him die tonight.

An hour later he was praying to those many deities to let him die.

Three hours after that they granted his wish.

9

The Mercedes SUV was good and jammed in the snow all the way up to the wheel wells.

When Levon came upon it, the Merc was grinding away, wheels spinning enough to make it shimmy side to side along the verge of the ring road that circled the lake. All the driver was accomplishing was digging the wheels in deeper.

He pulled his Ram up in front of it and climbed out. The driver was a woman of 30 or more. Pretty, with short-cropped pale, almost white, blonde hair. She wore what looked like a very expensive parka over a black turtleneck.

"Stuck?" he said.

"I should say." She smiled and her face colored a bit. There was a trace of an accent. The Merc's plates were Massachusetts but that wasn't it. Clipped and precise with no dropped consonants.

"I can turn around and winch you out."

"I think I'd only get stuck again. And you're the first person to come by in over an hour," she said.

He stepped back as she opened the door and stepped

out after raising the window. She wore leather boots with jeans tucked in. Both looked as pricey as the parka.

"Then I can give you a lift. You're on the lake?"

"Yes. The Moulson's house. They're letting me stay there while I do some work. Though I wish they'd been more strident in their warnings about Maine winters."

"What did they tell you?"

"That I'd freeze my ass off!" she said, and a laugh exploded from her.

He allowed a smile.

"I thought that was just an expression!" She laughed again.

"Well, my truck is warm, and I know where the Moulson place is," he said and held an arm out for her to take.

She blinked at the offered elbow before putting her arm in his and allowing him to walk her to his truck through the calf-deep drift she'd created around her car.

"I take it from your accent and manners that you are some kind of Southern gentleman," she said as he guided her. The boots she wore were fancy, but the slick soles were not made for travel in snow.

"Just an Arkansas redneck, ma'am," he lied.

"Ma'am? Call me Lee, please."

"I'm Mitch Roeder," Levon lied once more.

He helped her into the cab of the truck and crossed in front of the cab to climb behind the wheel and take off.

The Ram followed Mohawk, the road that ran around the circumference of Lake Bellevue. The locals still called it Gourd Lake for its shape: fat and oval at its southern base, narrowing to a neck that led to another, smaller span of water to the north. The developer who'd subdivided the parcels all around renamed it for the nearest town, a flyspeck along the county road ten miles east. Cecile's place was the only landmark. A gas station and combination convenience-and-hardware store that also served as the local post office, backed by a few homes owned by lifetime Mainers. Bellevue was a misleading name Anglicized from what was probably a joke name given it by the original French settlers. The only view the town offered was pine forest for hundreds of miles in every direction.

The twenty-two homes distributed around the lakeshore ranged from mini mansions to full-blown palaces. They belonged to financiers, a retired senator, a television producer, three trial lawyers, a construction contractor from Boston, a software developer from San Francisco, and a handbag designer from Italy. They were empty in the winter except for a few guests here and there. That meant they were empty most of the year since Maine winters tended to start early and then stubbornly hang on when the rest of the country was starting to wear t-shirts. They were boarded up and shut down, running only enough electricity to keep the pipes from freezing. The boats were out of the water and locked up in boathouses until spring. Pools were drained and all the toys put away.

"You don't seem to be having any trouble navigating through this," Lee remarked as the Ram rolled along easily, following the buried roadway through the trees.

"Your Merc is good in light snow. But it just doesn't have the clearance for this kind of depth."

"If I'd known that, I could have saved some money and bought a truck like this. Appearances over practicality has always been my downfall." She sighed.

He had nothing to say to that.

"I went down to Bellevue to buy some things I needed. Do you believe that they don't get any newspapers until the beginning of April? The woman behind the counter suggested that I Google whatever I needed to know. It's the only store still open, so I suppose I have to put up with that colorful character until the snow melts."

Levon had no remark for that. Cecile down at the Bellevue Market and Hardware *was* colorful.

"And what brings *you* to stay in this godforsaken place in the dead of winter? I'm doing some writing and so crave isolation. Though not so much isolation as this," she said.

She wanted a conversation.

"I have a place on the other side of Mohawk Road. Not right on the lake. It was a carriage house once."

"That tells me where but not why, Mitch."

"I'm doing some renovation work on one of the lake houses. Putting in a new kitchen. The family wants it done for when they come back up from Boston in the summer."

"So you have work to while away the dreary winter months as well. It must be lonely. God knows *I'm* lonely. Is there anyone else living around here?" she said with a gesture of exaggerated desperation.

"There's the Fentons. They work on contract for the home association. Danni does light maintenance like watering plants and making sure the pipes don't freeze. Nate looks after the heavier stuff like repairing furnaces and keeping generators running during outages."

"A gay couple?" She arched an eyebrow.

"Danielle. They have two kids. Carl and Giselle."

"Where do they live?"

"There's a guest cabin on the Morgan property. The rent's paid by the association. It's on the west side of the lake up near the neck."

"Anyone else?"

"The Espositos. Retired couple from Boston. They're in the east side of the neck a couple of properties north of you. And a pair of artists in the bungalow behind the Christophers. That's next door to you. That's about all."

"And you?"

"Our house is at the foot of the lake across the road from the Hofferts. The house I'm renovating."

"'Our?' Is there a Mrs. Redneck and a trailer full of little Rednecks?" She chuckled to let him know she was being playful.

"My daughter Moira. Her mom passed a few years back." The best lies always had some truth in them.

"Pity. Your poor little girl."

"It's been tough. But she's brave for my sake. Here's the Moulson's," he said and pulled off the road, following the tracks the Benz had left upon leaving to the bank of doors that fronted the six-bay garage that stood separate from the vast chalet-style mansion.

"I cannot thank you enough, Mitch," she said, climbing down from the cab.

"I can pull your SUV out and tow it here if you like."

"There's no hurry. I'm certainly not going out again any time soon and—what an idiot!" she said in a sudden shout.

He blinked at her.

"Oh, not you, my dear. I left everything I bought in Bellevue in the back of the car. The very reason I left the house in the first place," she said, slapping her hands against her sides.

"You head on in. I'll run down and get them for you," he said.

"You *are* a Southern gentleman." She beamed and closed the passenger door.

He watched her slip slide her way to the front door before following the circle drive around and back to Mohawk Road toward the snowbound Merc.

Something to write about.

10

The call at four in the morning found Nancy Vargas awake.

She was in bed with a laptop open atop a pillow across her thighs and a second open beside her where her husband used to sleep before he took off with an intern at his lobbying firm. Her red hair was pinned atop her head like Pebbles Flintstone. Her mom was Irish and her dad a Chicano. She told people she was a Micksican.

This hunt for the Blanco cash was keeping her up nights, which was way better than lying awake all night, hands fisted in the sheets and thinking of Rick fucking that graduate school bitch at her apartment in Georgetown.

Nancy's cell sang the opening the bars of a Pogues song. A number in Sydney appeared on the screen above a selfie of a grinning bearded man.

"You sound awake." Dave McCracken, a wonk at the Taxation Office in Oz that she'd met at a conference in London three years back. A member of the loose network of forensic accountants she'd dubbed the Legion of Super Beancounters.

"I *am* awake," she said.

"You sent out a profile of a robbery in Costa Rica a month back. Is that still something you're keen on?"

"It is."

"A home invasion-style burglary in Fiji came in that matches a lot of the details in your profile."

"What can you send along?" she said, already tapping keys, Googling "Fiji," "burglary," "home invasion" and "Corey Blanco."

"The official reports and a video of the crime scene. I'm trying to get a full forensic report as well. How's that for service, eh?" Dave said. She could tell he was smiling as he said it. The man had some serious dimples going on.

"Beautiful, Dave. You know where to send them. Thanks so much."

"I need to hear the magic words, love."

"'But I have no idea where these came from,'" Nancy said in a little girl singsong that brought an explosion of laughter from the other side of the world.

She moved to the desktop at her workstation in the living room and opened the files from McCracken. The video showed a crime scene similar enough to the home invasion at Puntayamas to give her *déjà vu*. The safe hidden behind the mirrors of the home gym. The two victims duct-taped into kitchen chairs and facing one another. They'd been in situ for a while indicated by the bloating and the presence of insects. They were only found when a groundskeeper crew followed a thick band of ants from a flower bed to a set of French doors with a clear view of the murder scene.

A young man with dark skin and longish black hair seated across from a young blond woman.

The woman was naked except for the plastic bag drawn tight about her head by her final inhalations.

Other than this she was untouched. The male was less fortunate. Close-ups in sickening high-definition detail showed where fingers and toes had been snipped off, probably by bolt cutters, as the examination of the children at the Costa Rican house had revealed. Teeth were pulled, the gums swollen and black. There were areas of severe burns to the chest from a torch or open flame. Nancy moved the cursor to take her back to the beginning of the video as the camera moved down to the man's genital area.

Screen captures of the home gym showed the open vault. They had drilled and tapped into the lock mechanism. No help with the combination this time. The job was neat, very professional. These guys were not pikers. They meant business. The broken mirror glass all about the room was the only sign that they were losing patience with the hunt.

In the vault they'd found slim pickings. Some cash and a single box containing envelopes of uncut gems.

She zipped past the homicide scene footage to a sequence where the goods from the vault were laid out on a table. Australian and US dollars in two-thousand-dollar bundles. She froze the image and counted about two hundred thousand in Oz money and a bit more in American. The gems were uncut diamonds that, if she was any judge, would trim down to two to three carats. Fifty-two of these in paper envelopes arranged in a velvet lined box. Three passports showing pictures of Corey Blanco, his trophy wife and their oldest child, the girl, at maybe three years of age. All with different names than the passports they'd found at the Puntayamas house. Ladies and gentlemen, meet Mr. and Mrs. Milton Van Schiver and their daughter Lainie.

So they hadn't visited this house in a decade. Not

since their youngest was born. How many other bolt holes did Blanco have around the world?

Her own digging revealed that the property in Costa Rica was purchased by a company incorporated in Cambodia. The construction of the house had been financed through a bank in Venezuela and paid off in full by a draft from a Bahamian bank from an account held by a limited partnership formed in South Africa and administered by a law firm in Johannesburg. Never anywhere on any document in all those transactions, settlements, or draws did Courtland Ray Blanco's name appear.

The place in Fiji would have a similar provenance. She was sure of it.

But did the crew find what they were looking for in this most recent invasion?

Nancy turned to the crime report that she printed up so she could read it from the comfort of her sofa. The FPF reports were dry reading but loaded with details. The robbery crew had left nothing behind by way of evidence. Not so much as a single shoe print. There was some DNA evidence still out but that held little promise as there were signs that all surfaces around the site of the vault and the two homicides were wiped. Someone even vacuumed the floor and furniture and took the vacuum cleaner with them when they left. Sadistic yet thorough.

Fingerprint evidence revealed that the male victim was a Fiji native of mixed Fijian and Asian Indian extraction. Further evidence indicated that he had been squatting in the house for an extended period of time. His prints were multi-layered and showed up everywhere in the house. The female was a German national from Rostock and fresh off a cruise ship that departed Fiji a week ago without her.

The detective who prepared the reports shared in the

notes his surmise that the villains (his words) unsuccessfully tortured the male, believing that he knew the combination to the vault. Both victims were then murdered when he failed to cooperate for whatever reason. Some consternation was expressed over the amount of cash and valuables left behind by the robbers. The conclusion reached by the primary detective was that the robbers were after something far more valuable, and left behind items that could later be traced to them.

The guy was half right.

Nancy knew that the invaders mistakenly believed that the German girl was housesitting and had some connection to the owners because she was the one who served as a witness. The Fijian squatter was the torture subject in an attempt to get her to talk. In the end, neither of them knew anything. In addition to being sadistic fucks, the robbers were also racist; assuming the white girl was in charge and the person of color only there for the scenery.

There was more about semen found on and in the person of the German but none of the usual signs of sexual assault. The sperm was a DNA match for the male victim. The local was using the Blanco hideaway as a fuckpad. Too bad, buddy. You picked the wrong house to hole up in. She felt sorrier for the girl. On a dream vacay on an island paradise and waking up to hell.

A glance at the clock. Only 6:30 AM. She wanted to call Bill Marquez and share all of this. But she was sure he wouldn't be awake for another few hours California time. She needed to calm down in the meantime. She stepped out onto the balcony off her apartment and shivered in the damp cold of Arlington in January. She lifted the dome cover off the barbecue grill and retrieved the crumpled pack of Kools she'd hidden there back when she and Rick quit together. How romantic. If he could cheat with that chippie, then she could have a cigarette now and then.

She hugged her cardigan about her and smoked and thought. Did the villains (that word was growing on her) get what they wanted? Was Fiji the end of the trail? Was there a way to determine the timeline of when the vault was drilled open and when the unlucky pair died? Were they tortured for the combination or afterward for revenge? Or maybe they asked the German girl where whatever the hell they were looking for was when they found the cupboard bare. She didn't know. She didn't know anything. That had to be clear to the robbers early on. No one can totally fake ignorance in the face of that kind of horror. And the poor *fräulein* from Rostock did not have an easy out like a weak heart to take her away from the monsters the way Corey Blanco had managed.

Then the hours of torture were retribution; someone taking out their frustration at being disappointed by what they found in the vault. That told Nancy two things.

They were still out there somewhere looking for their prize.

And someone on the crew enjoyed inflicting pain.

It was near 7:00 AM when she came back inside after two Kools.

Fuck it. Marquez would just have to stand an early wake-up. She found his cell number and tapped send.

11

The Celestron telescope was trained on the house directly across the lake. Rambling along the shore over a one-acre footprint, it looked more like a theme park attraction than a billionaire's summer home. A Swiss-style chalet with a faux-wood shake roof and eaves dripping with gingerbread wood trim sprawled atop another half-acre of terraced deck with steps to a boat dock. She could picture Julie Andrews skipping around the place followed by a gaggle of blond-headed kids in lederhosen and dirndls.

More money than style, Lee mused to herself and raised her eye from the rubber socket of the scope. Next to it and also aimed out the lake-facing bay window was a Nikon camera mounted with a telescopic optical cannon equipped with night vision atop a tripod and fixed in position. It was set to take time-lapse video in case she dozed off.

Her circadian rhythms were flipped. She slept most of the day and spent her nights checking the house across the lake for lights or sign of movement. Sometimes she shifted the view to take in the few neighbors that shared Mohawk Road with her.

There was a lot of downtime. The dangers of being bored to death seemed real to her. She cooked complicated meals in the gourmet kitchen and worked them off in the well-equipped home gym. She stayed fit as well by using a pair of in-track skis that she used to explore trails around the lake.

The Moulson house offered other distractions. An extensive library of Blu-rays and DVDs. They leaned to recent blockbusters and family-oriented fare except for the porno stash she found hidden in the back of the walk-in off the master bedroom. Lots of girl-on-girl which held little interest to her.

Snooping through the Moulsons' belongings occupied her for the first week she spent in their house. She learned quite a bit about them from her explorations. The information could come in handy should anyone ask her about them. It wasn't as if she knew them at all. She'd found the house by a search of real estate sites and county records. The Facebook page of their middle daughter (they had four children, three daughters and a son) mentioned her glee that Mummy and Daddy would be wintering in the house in the Bahamas until late February. The middle daughter was the wildest of the Moulson kids as well as the most open on social media about family comings and goings. With the parents away, the main Moulson domicile in Wellesley would be party central until their return.

Of the four homes Lee reconned, the Moulson place was the most ideally suited, being directly across from the house that held her interest. On paper, that house belonged to Downeast Holdings as a lease property. In reality, she knew it belonged, through several more stratum of shell companies, to a family named Blanco.

It was late in the day. The lowering sun created a persistent glare off the ice that was lancing into her eyes to kindle a migraine. To hell with that, she thought. They wouldn't come in the day anyway. And she knew they would come.

Lee went into the kitchen to help herself to an espresso from the excellent Jura machine she'd gotten so much use out of. A noise from the front of the house turned her away from the kitchen to the front foyer. Through the beveled glass windows to one side of the double front doors she could see the Ram truck of the man who'd helped her home the other day. The truck pulled up into the drive and turned into the half circle turnaround set before the front. Her Mercedes was behind it on a tow line. She could see someone behind the wheel of her Merc but could not make out any features through the tinted glass.

The Ram came to a rest and the man from the day before climbed from the cab. Mike? Mark? He went to the rear of the truck to undo the tow line. He was joined by a young girl in a bright yellow parka and a colorful toque with a long tail and tassel who got out of her car. He'd mentioned a daughter.

Lee slipped on an anorak and Uggs and opened the door to call to them.

"I'm just making espresso, and I think I see someone who'd like a hot chocolate," she called to them. The man hesitated and turned to speak to the little girl who grinned and nodded.

They joined her at the kitchen table. Moira was introduced. Lee had recalled Mitch's name by the time they reached the door.

Levon politely sipped a bit of the espresso while Merry munched a scone and drained a big mug of cocoa sprinkled with mini marshmallows.

"You didn't need to bring my car back. It's not like I'm going anywhere until the thaw," Lee said.

"I wanted to get it off the road for you. It was almost drifted over. Someone was going to run into it sooner or later." Mitch shrugged.

"A drunken hunter," the little girl offered.

"Well, I appreciate that," Lee said.

"Are you stocked for the winter? Even one person can go through a lot of goods," Levon asked.

"I believe I am. I mean, I think so. The Moulsons' have quite the larder. I don't remember when I've eaten so well."

"We make at least one trip to the Bellevue market every week," the girl said, licking away a chocolate mustache.

"We'd be glad to pick up whatever you need. That Cecile *has*, I mean," Levon said. He'd pulled a felt-tip pen from a pocket of his coat and looked around the counter for something to write on.

"That would be an enormous help if you could." Lee pulled a note pad from a drawer and placed it before him. Levon wrote their number on the top sheet by their new name. Roeder.

"We'll leave you to whatever you were doing, Miss…"

"It's Tessler. But please call me Lee, both of you," she said, and took his hand as well as the notepad in her own. A big hand, with a thick layer of callus on the edge and heel.

"Thanks for the cocoa," the little girl said and hopped from the chair to rush to the door.

"And the coffee," Levon said, meeting Lee's eyes with his own as took his hand back and made to follow his daughter.

"Any time," Lee said.

She went to the door to watch the two of them climb

into the cab of the truck. He held the door for the little girl and secured it shut behind her. As he rounded the front of the Ram he looked toward the house once more and saw Lee standing in the door regarding him. He dipped his head in acknowledgment before he got behind the wheel.

There might just be more ways to kill time in this barn other than DVDs and Pilates, she thought as she watched the truck turn away down the drive for the road.

———

Fifth Entry
12/27

Thought of A today.
I miss her.
Miss a lot of people. Lost a lot. I remember their names but not their faces.
Except for A.
I can see her face. I can smell her. I can feel her hand on me and mine on her.
The memories hurt. Maybe I should try and forget but I can't. Don't think I would if I could.
She's in my heart.
She always will be.

They spent New Year's Day at the Fentons.

The two Fenton kids were out on the ice with Merry, showing her the finer points of cross-country skiing. Small, colorful shapes on the flat white dish of the lake. Levon stood by the bay window of the cabin watching them. The Fenton boy and girl moving easily over the bright snow in easy rhythm. Merry making more halting progress; getting hung up and leaning on the poles to get going again. The Fenton girl made a herringbone turn to glide back to Merry and offer advice. Levon couldn't see their faces over the distance. Their body language told him they were laughing.

"Good kids," he said to himself.

"What's that, Mitch?" Danielle said from the kitchen.

"You have a good pair of kids. They're patient with my girl," Levon said, turning to her.

"Moira's so sweet. This is the first winter in a while they've had anyone near their age staying here."

"Are those black-eyed peas?" Levon watched her stir a bubbling pot with a wooden spoon.

"Sure are. I read that greens and black-eyed peas are a

Southern tradition for the New Year. Is that right? It's a good luck thing?"

"All my life. But where'd you get greens way up here?"

"Cabbage will have to do. Hope you don't mind a little Yankee food mixed in." Danielle smiled, raising a lid on a large stockpot with a pork butt steaming nestled in chopped green and red cabbage.

"Damn Yankees." Nate Fenton grinned as he entered the room from the rear of the cabin. His arms were loaded with neatly cut lengths of cordwood retrieved from the mudroom. Levon helped him stack the split logs in a wrought iron cradle by the stove set in the stone fireplace.

"Warm fire. Cold beer. And football on the TV," Nate said, crouching to poke a few logs atop the collapsing pile within the blazing stove.

Levon said nothing.

"You hunt much, Mitch?" Nate stood after closing the stove hatch, dogging it closed.

"When I was a kid. Not so much as I grew up," Levon said.

"Me neither. Some small game with my dad. Birds mostly."

"Uh huh," Levon said. He watched the kids moving easily over the lake. He couldn't pick Merry out for the three. She was moving like the Fenton kids, picking up skills.

"So, you know guns, Mitch?"

"Some."

In the kitchen, Danielle sighed.

"He wants to show you his rifle." She smiled.

Nate grinned, coloring.

"Boys and their toys," Danielle said as Nate led Levon from the room.

Nate drew the rifle from a canvas sleeve he pulled

from the back of a closet in the largest bedroom. An SKS semi-auto rifle. Chinese manufacture. The yellow wood stock was heavy. The metal finished in a dull black. It was complete with the fold back bayonet with a wicked triangular blade secured beneath the barrel by a hinge. It was oiled and well-maintained.

"I have five hundred rounds for it. Picked it up at a gun showdown in Augusta. Cleaning kit and everything," Nate said.

"Not for hunting," Levon said, running a hand over the smooth lacquered foregrip.

"For, you know, whatever. You never know, right?"

"You never know." Levon handed it back.

"I mean, late at night, there's only like eight state cops patrolling this whole state. From Moose Island to Portland. Eight cops."

"You expecting trouble, Nate?"

"You must think I'm some kind of nut, right? I just feel better knowing this is here." Nate shrugged and slid the rifle back into its sheath.

"You know how to shoot it?"

"I shot it some over the summer. I guess I'm good enough up close. You should think of getting something if you don't already." Nate closed the closet door.

"Maybe I will," Levon said, following the other man back toward the smells from the kitchen.

———

Seventh entry
1/3

Moose in the woods today.
Went out to the truck for something and they were standing in the driveway.

A bull and cow. Quiet as statues. Watched each other a while. They moved off without a sound.
Quiet for animals that big.
I dreamt about them. I hope that means something.

13

Watching himself on the big screen was like an out-of-body experience for Kosai Duong.

Not a near-death experience. More like a near-sex experience.

From his place, naked and firmly strapped into an occasional chair with bands of plastic tape, he faced the two-meter-wide screen with eyes wide.

There in radiant high definition was a video taken from a camera that had been obviously mounted in the ceiling of the master bedroom of this same hotel suite. Two slender young bodies, one a boy and one a girl, were gently touching the chubby body of a man tied by wrists and ankles to the bedposts by cording. The man was bathed in sweat and writhing; muted exclamations sounded from his nostrils since his mouth was securely fixed with a ball gag. The boy and girl worked over him using hands, lips, and tongues with most extraordinary deftness.

The chubby man was Kosai. This was what he'd paid ten thousand Thai baht for just last night. About five hundred Euro. He had no regrets.

Not, at least, until he was wakened by two uninvited guests in his suite at the Bangkok Hilton.

One man, an enormous blond Viking bastard, plucked Kosai from the bed as if he was a child then placed him in the chair and wound tape about his torso, wrists, and legs with practiced ease. The other man was smaller but frightened Kosai more. He was thinner with one milky, unmoving eye. The eye was a malignant, glittering jewel set on the plane of the man's face that appeared to droop. It looked to Kosai like the flesh was wax and had been allowed to melt a bit and then set that way permanently.

The man with the white eye operated the DVD player to replay the events of the night before. Watching the man's hands tab keys on the remote, Kosai realized that both men were wearing latex gloves. He looked down to see that their shoes were covered in white covers such as he'd seen surgeons wear in hospitals.

Kosai lost control of his bladder. The spray splashed the Viking's pants, earning Kosai a sharp slap across the back of the head.

"You are the Vice President of Operations for the Cambodian firm of Meas Phy Holdings headquartered in Phnom Penh." A statement rather than a question. It was spoken in competent French with an accent Kosai did not recognize. Kosai had learned French at university and spoke like a Parisian.

"I am," Kosai said. His voice was made feeble by fear. He fought to keep a smile of professional interest on his face. This was, after all, a business deal in the end. And it was quite clear to him what the stakes were.

"I am going to repeat a list of names. You will explain your relationship with these persons and organizations."

"As best I can." Helpful smile.

"Roostook Ltd."

"Yes. A South African law firm we do business with on that continent." A matter of public record.

"Scotiabank, Nassau."

"Ah. Our accounts in the Bahamas." Not a matter of public record.

"Banco Centro Internacional."

"Caracas. We do transfer funds through them." Funds no one but a handful of people know about.

"Standhope Securities."

Kosai swallowed hard. He nodded.

"Courtland Ray Blanco."

Kosai fought to keep the smile on his face. His face resembled that of a fish lying on the ice at a market stall. Frozen and without joy.

"That. That is very privileged information," Kosai managed.

"Which is why we come to you. You will allow us access to files on your network. Files that have so far defeated our efforts to decrypt them." The man with the half-melted face held Kosai's smartphone up to him in latex encased fingers.

"Or what?" Kosai regained some of his composure.

"Or this will be more than just a private show for the three of us," the wax-faced man said, gesturing to the big screen where the naked and sweating Kosai was arched, straining against his bonds like a wild thing with the two wickedly inventive children bringing him to ecstasy.

Kosai laughed at that. His restored composure turned to confidence. The world was a board room. They were negotiating. He had what they wanted. And, even from the weak bargaining position of being helpless in the hands of rough men, he had the upper hand. He had the keys to the encryption they sought to break.

"Who will you show it to? Members of the board? They will laugh. They will see me as a stallion. You think that they do not know what a business trip to Bangkok really means? That they have not come here for just this sort of adventure?"

The not-French man's functioning eye showed no more change than its dead white counterpart.

"Or my wife? You think she has a right to judge me? To embarrass me? Divorce me in Cambodian court?" Kosai spoke in a mocking tone. He would give these men nothing.

The man was poised before Kosai to tap the keyboard on the smartphone.

"Who will you show it to?" Kosai's professional smile turned to a grin.

"Your mother."

Kosai's face fell.

———

The sixteen-character passphrase tapped onto the tablet by Kosai's shaking fingers activated an algorithm that opened the secret world of Meas Phy Holdings' transactions and communications. Further passwords opened gates in firewalls to reveal a tapestry of foreign bank transactions leading, finally, to real estate properties held around the world under the name Rio Plaza del Rey— the code word the corporation assigned to the holdings of Corey Blanco.

Kosai's body was not found for three days. He floated up onto the banks of a canal off the Chao Phraya. Hauled from the muddy water and placed at the morgue for a week before he was identified as a major player in the cutthroat world of business in Southeast Asia.

And that is precisely how he ended his career. His throat cut.

Official reports in the media blamed his death on the

many dangerous street gangs that prowl Bangkok preying on tourists and visiting businessmen.

No mention was made of the shining DVD disc that hung from a piece of cording about his neck or the missing fingers and toes obviously removed by a mechanical device. And nothing in the reports mentioned the television remote found inserted deep in his rectum.

His mother burned joss sticks and prayed before his picture in the family shrine.

His wife salved her loss in the comfort of a luxury condo in Singapore, purchased with the insurance settlement left her by Kosai.

———

Ninth entry
1/6

Keeping a promise to myself to make an entry every day.
Work going slow on the kitchen. Have till spring to finish
— no need to rush it.
M doing well with schoolwork. Might have to skip her a
grade in Sept.
Snow stopped for a while.

———

Tenth entry
1/11

Summer residents are gone but we still have neighbors.
The woman at Moulsons.
The artist couple in the bungalow behind the
Christophers.

The Fentons.
The Espositos. He's a retired contractor. She's a talker.
They tell me it's too cold to snow any more.

14

"I hope you didn't pack for Fiji," Bill Marquez said from the monitor via Skype.

"Yeah. Treasury's not going to spring for tickets either." Nancy Valdez shrugged.

It was weeks since she'd woke him up with news of the break-in and murders in Fiji. They'd put their heads together and came up with the skeleton of a report using the evidence from both crime scenes to prove beyond any doubt that they were the work of the same crew. Nancy wrote hers up for her supervisor at Treasury, emphasizing the big boodle of stolen funds still lying out there somewhere forgotten and untaxed. Bill wrote up his own file, highlighting the heinous nature of the crime and even managed to put a national security spin on it for the Bureau.

Both reports drew scant interest and both agents were reassigned. The Costa Rica file was still active at the Bureau but in a kind of bureaucratic limbo, getting colder all the time. The Fiji crimes were treated as a non-incident because no American citizen was involved—

conveniently ignoring the connection to Corey Blanco that Nancy firmly established.

Her digging established that the construction of the Fiji house was financed by the same Cambodian corporation as the house in Costa Rica. The land it sat on was leased in perpetuity by a corporation registered in Delaware through a post box in Amsterdam. The financing was handled by the same two banks involved in the Costa Rican house except for this time it was the Bahamian bank that secured the loan and an account at the Venezuelan bank that made the payoff. And both accounts were held by Roostook Ltd in Johannesburg. Cute. The cards were reshuffled but it was the same deck of cards.

If that incredible flock of coincidences didn't tie both places to Corey Ray, then the personal items found at the Fiji house solidly confirmed the identity of the owner. Photos, a child's crayon scribbles, and some sex tapes that featured the Blancos in happier days and were, quite frankly, boring.

All received the big ho-hum at each of their respective agencies.

"Too bad we couldn't turn up anyone named Muhammed," Bill said more than once.

They were both assigned to other cases but stayed in regular contact over the Blanco case. Several times a week, on off-duty hours or when they could snag some time at their offices when the time zones overlapped, they compared anything they may have found. As time passed the discovery of new evidence petered away and the theorizing increased to form the bulk of their conversations.

"There's no video of anyone who might be in this crew anywhere. Not at airports or seaports or anywhere.

No rental cars. No nothing that can't be accounted for," she said.

"I know. I've watched the videos. Hours of surveillance videos looking for the same faces in both places," he said.

"They entered both places illegally. Easy peasy since the target houses were on the water."

"And in areas thick with pleasure craft."

"But that still begs a question," she said.

"It does, does it? Begs?" he said laughing at her turn of phrase.

"Sorry. I binge-watched two seasons of *The Tudors* over the weekend." She smiled.

"So, you *do* have a life."

"Such as it is, smartass. Back to my question. These guys just don't paddle ashore and wander around. They go right for their target by the shortest route, do their business and get out the same way. A few hours in and out with the bulk of that time spent torturing anyone they come across."

"Someone does their prep work. An advance man already on the island." Bill nodded.

"Someone who cases the place. Checks for alarms. Police presence. Who's home and who's not. Comings and goings. Other relevant data. The skids are greased for the team when they arrive on the scene like a rock band to take the stage," Nancy said.

"They also need to *locate* the targets, right? They'd need to do the same kind of digging you did to find any real estate holdings that Blanco finagled."

"I don't think so, Bill. Maybe for the first house but not the Fiji house and not any others."

"What makes you say that?"

"Blanco died taking his secrets with him. But the wife

was still alive, and I have to think she'd share anything she knew to make them stop doing what they were doing to her kids."

"Like tell them about any other possible hiding places."

"That's probably the only thing she knew. Blanco kept everything else a secret from her. But she damn sure knew where they lived, what houses they owned," Nancy said.

"And she traded that," Bill said.

"Wouldn't you?"

"If I had kids. Yeah."

"So, the villains have a treasure map. They just don't know where 'X' is."

"Villains? Is that more of *The Tudors*?"

"Just something I picked up." She smirked.

"Well then I beg the question, *is* there a next place and, if there is, *where* is it?" he said, rubbing his chin with his fingers.

"Beats the shit out of me, G-man."

———

Fourteenth entry
1/15

Still dreaming. Same shit. More recent stuff mixed in.
Stuck here with no distractions.
Had a movie night last night at the Hofferts.
Just the two of us in a media room bigger than my parents' old house in Needham.
Something with raccoons.
M liked it. Laughed a lot.
She's tough. I know she misses her mother. She never talks about her.

Maybe I should start talking more.
But I can't.
Wind's picking up.
They tell me that means more snow.

15

"Don't you have any more Archies?" Merry said.

"Just what's here. The Greenbergs gave them to me before they left for Florida," Carl Fenton said.

The kids, including Giselle, were in the great room of the cabin that the Fentons called home. It had high ceilings, and everywhere Merry looked she saw gleaming yellow wood. It was like a place where a hobbit might live.

"This one continues next issue, and you don't *have* the next issue," Merry said, putting the comic back atop the short stack.

Giselle lay back on a daybed, engrossed in something on her tablet. "Is it the one where Archie can't decide between Betty or Veronica?" she said without looking up.

"That's the one. You read it?" Merry said.

"I don't have to. That's what they're *all* about," Giselle said, rolling her eyes before turning them back to the screen in her hands, thumbs working furiously.

"I have lots of Spiderman," Carl offered, shoving a cardboard box stuffed with comics across the table.

"Does he have a girlfriend?" Merry said, inspecting the cover of one she pulled from the upright stack.

"Sure. He's even married in some of them," Carl said, riffling through copies.

"Get me those ones," Merry said.

"Sure, Moira," Carl said and began assembling a selection for her.

The younger kids read while Giselle, far too mature for comic books at fourteen, texted friends and cursed the slow wi-fi she was borrowing from the nearest house, a Swiss nightmare of a place owned by some Wall Street guy.

A whining sound off the lake broke the muttered silence.

Merry broke off reading to go to the bay window through which she could see past the bigger house to the lake surface. It was blinding white even in the muted glare from the overcast sky.

"There's someone on the lake," Merry said.

Giselle joined her. Carl remained absorbed with his comics.

Out on the vast flat surface sat three tiny dark shapes. Giselle got a pair of binoculars from a drawer in the base of the bay window. They kept it there for moose watching. She focused then watched a while before handing it to Merry who was eager for a peek.

Through the lenses Merry could see that there were a pair of wooden shacks out on the ice where they had not been earlier that day. Parked behind them was a pickup bigger than her father's, with huge knobby tires fitted with chains. The door of one of the shacks opened and two men stepped out. They walked with a peculiar gait over to the second shack a hundred feet away. One of them carried a tool of some kind but it was too far for

Merry to see what it was. They both went into the second shack and the whining noise started up again.

"What are they doing?" Merry asked Giselle.

"They're going to piss my dad off as soon as he sees them."

———

Nate Fenton *was* pissed off.

He aimed the snow machine toward the two ice fishing shacks and turned the throttle to race over the ice toward the two idiots hurrying back to their pickup. One of them fell hard on his ass as Nate drew up in front of the F-150 to block its escape. Dennis Walbrooke was helping his brother Tom up off the ice.

The two shacks were roughly the size of small walk-in closets. They were plywood over a wooden frame with tar paper roofs and holes cut for a stove pipe for propane-fueled heaters. They'd been lined inside with insulation covered by beaverboard panels to keep them cozy. They sat on two-by-fours that served as skis so the pickup could pull them over the ice at the end of tow chains.

"Do we have to do this every year, guys?" Nate said, cutting the engine and climbing off the saddle.

"What's a few fish, Nate?" Dennis said. Tom braced himself against the bed of the Ford to regain his balance.

"When they're fish that don't belong to you? You know Ty Grant stocks this lake with trout every year. I'd think he'd expect a few left over for himself when he puts his line in come spring," Nate said and leaned on the truck himself.

"Aw come on, champ," Tom Walbrooke groused.

The three had gone to school together. Dennis a year

behind and Nate and Tom in the same grade until Tom ran into Algebra and dropped back to join his little brother. Nate was something of a local hero for making all-state as a wide receiver for Arundel Regional High.

"Yeah, those fish spend all winter under the ice fucking each other and making more little fishies. There's plenty for all, Nate." Dennis pleaded the same argument he had last year and all the years before since Nate had taken on the job as a caretaker for the lake properties.

"It's not the little ones Grant is interested in, and you know that, you dumb shit," Nate said but he was smiling.

The brothers were encouraged by the smile and returned it with eager expressions.

"You'll have those shacks off by the first sign of thaw? And you'll keep your catch down to a reasonable number?" Nate said.

Both brothers nodded with enthusiasm, grins broadening.

"You're welcome any time to try your own hand, champ," Dennis said.

"That's very kind of you to invite me to poach along with you. But have either of you ever heard of deniability?"

The brothers exchanged an uncertain glance.

"That means I have to pretend I didn't see you." Nate sighed.

The brothers' grins refreshed, and they elbowed each other with great enthusiasm.

Before saddling up on the snow machine Nate turned to glance back at the cabin set above the road on the western bank. The sun gleamed off something at the faraway bay window. The kids were watching him at work. That made Nate smile. As he turned his head another glint flashed in his peripheral. A glare from one of the larger homes on the east shore. It was gone before he could fix its exact location. He cranked the engine to life and turned back west to the next house on his rounds, leaving the Walbrookes to finish drilling their second ice hole in the center of the lake.

16

The phone rang in the kitchen. Merry raced from her schoolwork to answer, the call a welcome distraction from a sheet of math problems.

"It's Lee!" she hollered, covering the phone mike with her hand.

"I didn't know who else to call, Mitch," Lee Tessler said when Levon picked up the cordless in the garage.

"Nate is the one who usually handles things like that," he said.

"He can't get to me until tonight. Something about a tree that came down overnight."

"I can come over and take a look."

"Would you?" she said, sighing with relief.

The problem was snow that had drifted up around the outdoor heat pump intakes, shutting down the four units that heated the Moulson house. Levon shoveled the snow away from them. Lee was leaning at a window inside the house, wrapped in a cardigan with a ski cap tilted on her head, watching him digging. He saw her there. When he had the units cleared all the way around, he made a stirring motion to her with a finger.

She disappeared from the window. The fans atop the heat pumps whirred to life. The defrost cycle would melt the remaining ice from the vent flanges. He turned to the window to see her motioning for him to come inside.

"Nate can put up a snow fence to keep that from happening again," he said, taking a mug of coffee from her.

"You didn't seem to be a big espresso fan last time. That's just regular old coffee," she said from the broad island at the center of the kitchen. She set the coffee carafe down on the granite top.

"It's fine," he said.

"And I mean *old*. I think the can of Maxwell House I found was here when the house was built."

"As long as it's hot."

"And thanks for coming by. I woke up this morning and I could see my breath. Jiggling the thermostat and calling the super is the extent of my expertise. I'm not used to winters like this."

"I thought you said you were from Boston."

"I leased the Merc in Boston. I live in New York. A condo. Twenty floors above the weather. Have a problem? Call maintenance."

"You have an unusual accent," he said.

"I blame the Hudson River Valley and northern boarding schools," she said.

"Yankee through and through." He smiled. She smiled back.

"Even so, these Maine winters are an entirely different animal."

"Are you regretting your decision to stay here?" He set the mug down.

"Actually, no. Can I top that off?" she said and came around the island to stand close by him to take the mug.

"Still a few swallows in there," he said touching her hand. She didn't move from his side.

"Like I was saying, there are a few good reasons for staying through the winter."

"The house is starting to warm up," Levon said, removing his fingers from the back of her hand.

"I know a way to make it even warmer. You know, I lied before. I never called Nate." She tilted her head, looking up at him from under a strand of hair come loose from under her cap. The corner of her mouth curved.

He stood to go. She touched the sleeve of his coat.

"Can't you think of a reason to stay a little while longer?" She removed the cap and her fine blonde hair fell about her shoulders.

"What kind of reason, Lee?"

"You're a man. I'm a woman. It's cold outside and warm inside." Her hand moved to his shoulder.

"Because I'm a man."

"You have a cock, don't you?"

"And that makes me a man."

"It sure helps, Mitch," she said. Her easy smile widened.

"I told Moira I'd only be a little while. I need to get back," he said, taking a step from her. Her hand dropped to her side. He picked up his coat from the seat back and moved toward the door.

"Do I need to apologize?" she said, following him.

"No need to apologize, Lee. For either of us," he said and was gone.

She watched him get in the truck and pull away, her breath misting the glass pane.

17

The bike messenger had never delivered to a park bench before. The waybill read in block letters:

MAN IN BLACK
THIRD BENCH FROM EAST
BEHIND DELACORTE THEATER
CENTRAL PARK

He was going to make a remark about it to the recipient until he saw the face of the man in the black raincoat rising from the bench to meet him. Half the guy's face looked like it was made of putty and left out in the sun too long. Without a word, the messenger handed over the 8"x5" padded envelope. The man took it in a gloved hand and turned to walk away.

"Hey, I need a confirmation signature," the messenger said. He pulled a tablet from the pocket of his parka.

"Ride away," the man said in a foreign accent that sounded like it came from the bottom of a grave.

"Okay then," the messenger said and pedaled away in the opposite direction.

Koning tore the package open as he exited the park onto Fifth Avenue. A cellphone slid into his hand. No note or message. The phone was fully charged. He pocketed it. He dropped the envelope into a trashcan.

It was later that night when the phone came alive with an insect buzz. Koning was in the piano bar of his hotel. A rather talented woman, still attractive in her late 40's, played standards in a soothing and assured manner. Koning hated being in the United States in general and New York City in particular. The city was vulgar and commercial. It had no personality. The black spots of chewing gum spat from a million mouths to form nasty constellations on the sidewalks repulsed him. The piano bar was as far as he cared to go from his room.

He dropped a twenty on the bar and walked out into the lobby and out onto 71st Street before tabbing the phone and lifting it to his ear.

"Koning?"

He said nothing.

"The line is secure, Koning. This phone is a virgin. We may speak openly." The voice spoke Dutch clearly but with a filthy accent. Javanese, perhaps.

"I do not know your name," Koning said. He stood in the nave of an office doorway. The street was quiet at this hour. A freezing rain kept Manhattanites indoors. The muted sound of thumping pop music could be heard from behind the garish neon façade of an Irish bar across the street.

"You know my money. In fact, you are quite free with it."

"And I will need more."

"This is becoming an expensive enterprise."

"Risk and reward. You are a businessman after all. You understood the odds. You know the prize is worth the investment," Koning said.

"Investment. How proper. I understand the concept of venture capital. I only remind you that I expect results," the voice on the other end of the phone said.

"This next target seems most likely. It was the most carefully hidden. That tells us something."

"Your people are with you? They are ready?"

"They are near the target." Koning's crew had arrived on the continent the day before. They were divided between Montreal and Toronto. The only exception was his advance element sent well ahead to gather the intelligence needed.

"And you need funds."

"There is special equipment we require."

"You cannot steal it?"

"Risk arrest for petty theft in pursuit of Aladdin's cave?"

"How much?" There was a chuckle in the voice.

"A million. Dollars. Part of that covers our exit."

"The getaway," the voice said in English, amused.

Koning said nothing.

When can I expect good news?" the voice said with growing impatience on the edges.

"Watch CNN. They will tell you when it is over."

"Good hunting, Koning."

The line went dead.

He opened the phone to remove the battery and SIM card. These he disposed of in two different dumpsters on his way back to the hotel. The body of the phone went down between steel grates in the sidewalk.

Koning shrugged off his raincoat and draped it over the back of his chair at the hotel bar. He gestured to the bartender for another gimlet of Stoli. The woman played the opening of "Easy to Love" in an easy tempo that came off the keys like treacle.

———

Fifteenth entry
1/16

Finished the electrics for the kitchen. Plumbing is next.
M spending more time with C and G.
She's begging for a sleepover. Maybe that's a good thing.
Time away from her gloomy old man.
Snow started after lunch. Wet snow.

18

The night of the sleepover, Danielle Fenton cooked enough spaghetti for an army. She insisted that Levon stay and eat with them.

"Where's Nate?" he asked, pulling up a seat at the table where the kids were already digging into a steaming basket of rolls.

"The artist couple called. Something about their hot water heater," Danielle said and lowered a huge ceramic bowl of pasta onto the table.

"Artists? What kind of artists?" Merry asked.

"I'm not sure. Painters, I think. Your father met them when they were moving in," Danni said around the oven mitt between her teeth.

"What did dad say they were like?" Giselle asked as she toured around the table grinding fresh parmesan on everyone's pile of pasta.

"He said they were hippies," Danni said, taking a seat opposite Levon.

"Hippies!" Giselle declared with a guffaw.

"Well, to your father, anyone who doesn't earn a paycheck is a hippie." Danni shrugged.

They passed around a milk pitcher that was doing duty tonight as a sauce tureen. This was followed by a platter of Danni's famous venison meatballs.

"The secret is, I grind the meat with just a little pork," she said as she encouraged Levon to spear a third meatball the size of a baseball.

"Then it's not really a secret," Levon said without a trace of a smile.

"I guess it's not. Now that I told you, I guess I'll have to kill you, Mitch," she said with an open smile.

Everyone laughed at that but Levon. He made the best smile he could and bent to his plate.

"Daddy calls them 'deer balls,'" Carl shared with a broad grin.

"Carl!" Danni cried.

The kids surrendered to a snuffling of barely suppressed giggles. Danni turned red and covered her mouth with a napkin to hide her smile.

After dinner, Levon made for a quiet departure. "Let you kids have fun," he said as he pulled on his coat at the door.

Merry burst across the room, leaping the board game they had laid out on the floor; world conquest in process. She hugged him about the waist, drawing him as tight as she could.

"What will you do without me?" she said into the rough canvas of his coat.

"I thought I'd read some of that Civil War book you gave me until I fall asleep," he said and touched her hair.

"Will you come have breakfast with us?"

"I might still be too full from Mrs. Fenton's meatballs. Besides, you'll probably sleep in."

"Okay," she said and released him.

"Love you, honey," he said.

"Love you back," she said.

Levon took the long walk to the truck, gunned it to life, and headed away out the drive before the cabin and onto Mohawk Road. He hooked a right. The distance back to his place was equal either way he went around the lake. He'd go around the east shore tonight, taking it slow over the mounting snow. A full-scale blizzard was in effect. A thirty-mile wind was blowing the white flakes against the truck like millions of tiny missiles. He drove with the fog lamps on and the fully lit rack of LEDs he'd installed on a bar above the cab.

He hadn't told Merry the whole truth. There was no way he was going to get any sleep with her out of the house. He decided to make a big old thermos of coffee and spend the night completing the plumbing to the Hoffert's new kitchen. By morning, he hoped to have the soil pipe connected and the PVC for the garbage disposal, dishwasher, and ice maker in place for when he installed the appliances still crated in the Hoffert's garage. The Civil War book Merry bought him was a very thoughtful gift but proved slow going for him as he stopped to think on the errors made by both sides. By the Union at the beginning of the war and by the Confederacy toward the end. Too many parallels. He'd see it through to the end, though, only because Merry gave it to him.

Levon decided that he would have rather fought under Lee than the Union. It wasn't just his Alabama heritage. Lee was the more talented commander and Levon had an affinity for lost causes.

He crawled by the bungalow behind the Christopher residence. The main house was a sprawling Cape Cod on a grand scale seated by the lake shore. The bungalow set across the road was a simple A-frame. The lights were on inside. Nate's snow machine sat at the foot of the drive. The toolbox sled he rigged up was hitched to the rear of it. Nate would be working on the water heater in the utility room down in the daylight basement. Levon thought about stopping to ask if he needed help but drove on. He was about talked out after the evening, even though all he did was mostly listen at the Fenton's dinner table.

The Christophers were a late middle-aged couple. He was legal counsel for an entertainment company in New York. She did something in the news for a television network. Neither of them seemed like the artsy type. Maybe the hippies, as Nate referred to them, were family friends.

Levon rolled on toward the Hoffert house, his mind moving to the problem of properly angling the soil lines in the constricted space left to him by the cabinet design the Hofferts had chosen.

––––––––

Eighteenth entry
1/19

M is away visiting. Funny how she fills the house somehow.
Going to work the kitchen some more.
Snow falling harder.
Wind picking up.
Two more feet by morning.

19

Nick Esposito thought his wife was crazy for wanting to come up to the lake house in the winter. He thought he was even crazier for agreeing to it.

"What's wrong with Florida?" Nick said.

"*Everybody* goes to Florida when it gets cold," Jessie said.

"You know there's a good reason for that," Nick said.

Here they were in deepest Maine, snowed in until Good Friday probably. Plenty of food in the freezers. Nothing for him to do but read, watch movies and, when Jessie wasn't watching, lose money playing online poker.

"What are you in the mood for?" Nick said. He was standing at the shelf system packed with DVDs.

"Whatever you'd like to watch," Jessie said, wrapped in a down quilt by the fire he'd built for them in the river stone hearth. The sweet smell of apple wood filled the room. Nick prided himself on the fires he could build.

"We have the last season of that show with the high school teacher cooking drugs on the side." He'd long ago stopped using titles for movies and shows since Jessie could never remember them. Instead, he had to give her one-sentence plot summaries.

"Oh, that show's awful." She winced.

He sighed.

"Pick something else," she said.

"We haven't watched that one with Pierce Brosnan in a while."

"Is he James Bond in it?" She made a face.

"It's the one you like where he's not James Bond. He steals a famous painting. You liked the actress's purse."

"An Hermès bag! Okay, we'll watch that if you want to." She beamed.

He'd watch anything as long as he could snuggle up to the hot toddy steaming in a mug on the coffee table.

They were forty minutes in. Jessie was enjoying the movie. Pierce Brosnan was enjoying Rene Russo. Nick was enjoying his second hot toddy, a warm buzz enveloping him just like the quilt his wife was wearing like a womb.

Lights flashed across the walls of the room. Nick muted the TV. Headlights came through the windows at the front of the house — someone pulling up the drive. A burring sound rose to overpower the voices from the television speakers.

"Who the hell's out in this?" Nick said.

"You'd better go see," Jessie said, taking the remote from his hand as he rose from the sofa.

A pair of snowmobiles were pulled up on the drive. Their engines rumbled and popped as they idled. Two men in black snowsuits and helmets. One dismounted and was crunching toward the front door.

"Can I help you guys?" Nick said from the open front door, eyes squinted against the pelting snow.

The dismounted man strode up the walk raising his arm, raising something in it to point at Nick Esposito.

A blinding flash wiped away the world. Nick was on the ground. He didn't remember falling. It was getting hard to breath. He tried to speak. Something warm and thick bubbled in his mouth.

The man in the black snowsuit stepped over him to walk in through the open door.

Nick tried to call out to Jessie. No sound came out. He was drowning in his own blood.

20

"Coffee or tea?" Lily said, poking her head into the utility room.

"Coffee would be great," Nate said. He was down on his knees working in the hatch at the bottom of the fat water heater tank.

"Decaf or regular?" Lily said.

"Regular black. Between this beast and the sleepover at home I'm not getting any sleep tonight anyway." He smiled and stood.

"Sleepover?" Lily said tilting her head. She had an accent. German, maybe?

"It's like a party," Nate said.

She nodded, pulling her head back and closing the door behind her.

Lily and Sascha. No last name. Funny couple. They were artists. Or at least they said they were. They never offered to show their work. Nate never saw any evidence of paints or sculpture anywhere in the house either tonight or when he was here back in the fall to introduce himself. That's when he arrived at his snap opinion that the pair were hippies. Sascha had a ponytail and a hipster goatee. Lily's kinky red hair always looked like she just got out of a wind tunnel. They both wore sandals with thick socks no matter what the weather was. They dressed in layers of 'natural' clothing. As the temps dropped, they looked like they were wearing every stitch they owned. Hippies through and through. No evidence of what kind of art they worked on, though. He asked just to be polite. They told him they didn't like talking about their 'process.' Fine with Nate. He didn't really want to hear about it anyway.

Nate pulled the heating elements from the floor of the tank. As he'd suspected, one of them was shot. A crack in the glass tube enclosing the corkscrew filament. Lucky for the hippies he had spares in the tool sled. A lot of the homes and guest houses were built by the same contractor — Tillottson Brothers down in Bangor. So most of the places had the same water heater. Nate kept plenty of spare parts on hand. Winters were hard on everything. The lifespan of a water heater up here was cut in half by six months of Maine's dry cold. A new element would hold them till spring and then the tank would need to be replaced.

He walked out through the open garage door down the drive to the snow machine and tool sled. The machine and sled were covered in an inch of new snow. It was still falling thick enough to make the world feel closed in to just the area around the bungalow. Danni called it the snow globe effect. The Christophers' old rambling Cape Cod across the road was a big gray heap. Beyond that the lake was invisible in a field of swirling white. There was no sound but his own breathing. It was as if Nate was on a spacewalk.

The spare elements were in one of the steel drawers

on his tool sled. Nate yanked and closed, yanked and closed until he found the row of boxes of new elements resting in the bottom drawer. As he rose from a crouch to trudge back to the house, he heard a noise cut through the silence.

A high whining sound. More than one sound. Check that — the same sound from multiple sources.

The snow and the trees combined to muffle and reflect the sound. The noise was coming from the north shore of the lake up near the top of the gourd's neck. Nate walked further up the drive to the bungalow. He stood trying to see the lake beyond the obscuring mass of the Christopher place. All he saw was the dense curtain of falling snow. The sound grew in volume as he listened.

"Mr. Fenton?"

Nate turned to see Lily standing inside the open garage with a steaming mug of coffee in her hands.

"I have your new element. I just heard something out on the lake," he said and crunched through the snow back to the garage.

"Heard something? What kind of something?" she asked.

"Sounds like snow machines. Thought it might be guys I know ice fishing. But even Dennis and Tommy aren't crazy enough to be out in this," he said, accepting the cup. Decorated with hand painted flowers. She tripped the button and the garage door rumbled closed.

"How long to fix the heater?" Lily said. She seemed impatient with him. Her eyes were narrow behind her glasses. Very un-hippie, he thought.

"Ten minutes to get the element back in. Give it an hour or so to get the tank filled in and back up to heat."

"Good. That is good," she said but didn't sound happy

about it. She popped back into the house, leaving him to his work.

He sipped the coffee.

It tasted like she put cinnamon in it.

Damn German hippies.

21

The kids finished up the game of *Risk*. Carl won by holding onto Afghanistan.

"He plays the same way every time. Loads up in Afghanistan and sticks to it no matter what." Giselle sighed.

The girls outvoted the boy for the next board game. *Life*.

The kids were in flannel pajamas. Despite the blazing fire going in the iron stove set in the fireplace, there was still a chill. They also wore wooly socks under their slippers and thick robes belted tight. Danielle Fenton got in the sleepover groove in a fluffy sky-blue robe with a pattern of leaping sheep. She busied herself serving up hot chocolate and refilling the community popcorn bowl set by the playing board.

Just as Merry was choosing college as her pathway to success the lights went out. The dishwasher went silent. Giselle's iPod dock died away in the middle of her favorite One Direction song. Near as Merry could tell, they were *all* her favorite song.

The kids ran to the windows facing the lake. It was

pitch dark but for the dull radiance of the lake surface visible through the gap between the house below them and the trees.

"All the houses are out," Giselle announced.

"Then it's not just us, right?" Carl said.

"That's right, genius," Giselle said.

Merry looked out through the haze of blowing snow. Her breath fogged the glass. The world outside looked like an underexposed photograph. The snow stood white against the black of the trees. The sky was low and dark.

Mom to the rescue. Danni appeared with candles, distributing them around the family room to make islands of light in the gloom. Carl was up and away into the dark. He came back, winding up a friction-powered camping lamp that threw the game table into high relief.

"Get that out of my eyes!" Giselle said. Carl stood on a chair and set the lamp in the curve of the hanging chandelier over the table. It cast a beam down on the table so they could keep playing.

"See how this is better than video games? The power goes out and you keep right on playing," Danni said. Like most everyone in Bellevue, the Fentons homeschooled. Like most homeschoolers, video games were verboten; too much of a distraction.

"Yes, Mom," both Fenton kids said in near unison. They didn't really miss playing *Supercart* or *Halo* since they'd never played anything like a video game, except for the three or four trips to Bangor to their aunt's house in the spring and summer. There an arcade in the back of their favorite pizza place. They *did* wish their mother didn't recite the same sermon every time there was an electrical outage. And they were frequent in the winter months.

Danni picked up the old wall phone in the kitchen and looked to the contact list of lake residents for the

Christopher's guest bungalow. Almost all the houses had landline phones. Bellevue was a half hour drive from any kind of cellphone coverage. She found the number and shouldered the phone to tap out the number.

The phone was dead. That was unusual. The phones always worked during other blackouts. There must be something serious going on down the line somewhere. Danni turned to the recharger on the counter. Both walkie-talkies were there. She'd just have to wait until Nate came back to find out what he knew about the electric.

"Thank God for the propane oven. There'll still be chocolate chip cookies," Danni proclaimed after replacing the phone in its cradle.

"Sometimes I think Mom likes these pajama parties more than we do," Giselle said.

The other two kids giggled at that.

Merry was pushing a carload of pink and blue pegs around the board and trying to catch up with Carl, who was looking like he'd make his second board game win of the evening. He had lots of cards and play money on his side of the board. All Merry had were cards saying she owed money on her school loan. How was this game fun again?

"I have to pee," she announced and hopped from her chair.

"But I was winning!" Carl carped.

"So go ahead and win," Merry said. She scooped up a candle holder from an occasional table and headed back toward the home's only bathroom.

She didn't really need to pee. She only needed a break. In the guttering light of the candle, she sat on the edge of the tub. She was bored with the game. It was making her angry at everyone and no one. Merry promised herself she wasn't going to cry even though she could feel her eyes growing hot at the corners.

Mr. and Mrs. Fenton were so nice, and she really liked Giselle and Carl. They wanted her to feel at home in their house. Seeing these people so happy and close and warm in their house only reminded her that she had no family of her own except her father. He had family in the northern part of Alabama but didn't talk about them much. Merry's mother passed away a long while back. Her grandma and grandpa died in some kind of accident. Daddy didn't talk about that much except to say that it was the reason they had to leave Alabama; the reason they had to change their names and never talk about themselves. Merry wanted to ask more but wasn't sure how much she wanted to know. At first it felt like playing real-life spies. More and more it just made her feel lonely. Having to lie to the Fentons and everyone else she met made her feel bad. Merry felt like she was hurting people that wanted to care about her, wanted to like her. And here she was hurting them with lies, and they didn't even know she was hurting them.

She stood up and flushed the toilet. The candle guttered and sparked then glowed brighter. Cold air blew in under the bathroom door. A crashing sound came through the wall. Then a high voice shouting and a long squeal. The bark of a male voice. No laughter followed.

Merry blew out the candle and pressed her ear to the bathroom door. She could hear talking. The deep voices of men speaking. Mrs. Fenton's voice rose up above theirs. Another crash of furniture and glass breaking. The shift and fall of heavy boots shuddered the floor-boards. She couldn't hear Mrs. Fenton anymore. Only the sound of men talking. She couldn't make out the words.

The bathroom was in the interior of the house. There were no windows to the outside.

Merry turned the doorknob as slowly and quietly as she could and pushed the door open only wide enough to see out through the gap with one eye. Shadows moved on the one wall she could see through the narrow slit. Shadows thrown dancing by the camping lamp set swinging in the chandelier. The men's voices kept on. They were calling to one another as they moved through the house from room to room. Merry couldn't make out any words. It sounded like a man giving orders and a couple of other men answering. They weren't police. There'd been no knock at the door.

She opened the bathroom door enough to allow herself to slip through. She stepped from her slippers to move without sound on her heavy woolen socks deeper into the house away from the voices. The corridor lined either side by Giselle and Carl's bedrooms ended in a mud room with access to the back of the house. Merry moved into the unheated room where the Fentons kept things like firewood, sleds, boots, and a big deep freezer standing silent against one wall. The cross-country skis Daddy gave her for Christmas leaned by other pairs of skis belonging to the Fentons. She searched for her boots among the neat row lined up on the concrete floor. Merry tied a quick knot in the loose ends of the laces and looped the boots over her shoulder. With the skis and poles cradled under one arm, she opened the back door off the mudroom, careful not to let the long skis scrape on the floor or jamb.

She plunged off the back stoop into knee-deep snow. She made her stumbling way into the trees away from the lights glowing from within the house. Her passage left a deep furrow with a parallel groove left by the dragging end of the skis behind her. The falling snow and lateral wind would fill them in. Even now the crusted top layer lay under a constant fog of blowing crystals driven by stiff gusts off the lake. All traces of her escape would soon be invisible so long as none of the men looked out back in the next few minutes.

The burden of the skis and poles was awkward in the thick snow. Her pace was slow as she moved for the sheltering darkness of the trees. She felt like, at any moment, a voice would call out behind her to break the stillness of the night. The lowest branches at the tree line were borne down into the drifts that had blown against them. She reached their sheltering cover on her hands and knees. Merry threw the skis and poles through a space between boughs and dove in after them.

The dark within the woods was near total and she gave herself a moment to adjust to the gloom. Closed her eyes tight the way her father taught her. Safe in the shadows of the trees, she leaned her back to a tree to pull on her boots. The cold reached through the wool of her socks to chill her feet. They were still dry. Struggling and hopping, she managed to slide the boots on and lace them up tight. She stepped into the traps on the skis, using the poles for balance. Merry lifted her legs one at a time and set the fastened skis on the surface of the snow. She was careful to distribute her weight as Giselle taught her and stood upright. Her footing was good now, a solid stance. She slid one ski forward followed by the other, balancing with the poles as she moved up to a steady pace between the trees away from the Fenton's cabin and through the absolute quiet of the woods to find her father.

22

Leandra, Lee to her friends, was busy at her laptop when the lights went out. The computer went to battery mode, going dim before recovering and washing the kitchen in blue light.

"Shit," Lee said.

Ten seconds later the generator somewhere at the back of the house growled to life. The big sub-zero refrigerator came back online as well as a few can lights in the ceiling. Lee went around the house cutting the lights out to conserve the gas in the generator since she had no idea how to refuel it. With the laptop held before her like a bulls-eye lantern, she searched the kitchen and adjoining great room for an outlet that still had juice provided by the generator. No luck.

She closed the laptop to save battery life. The room turned black but for the silvery glow off the snow coming in from the windows. It was enough light to allow her to navigate. The gas stove still worked, and she turned the flame on to heat water for tea.

With a steaming mug of Earl Grey, she took a seat on the cushions of the vast bay window that looked out over the lake. Fingers of cold bled through the double panes. Her hands were wrapped around the warm mug she held against the front of her cable sweater.

The lake lay like a platter of burnished pewter. The wind whipped the snow off the surface into shifting dunes. The caps of the white ridges turned to powder and streamed away in swirling patterns blown by the gale. The lights around the lake were gone. The houses were invisible against the black wall of the forest. It was easy to imagine that she was alone in all the world. For all practical purposes she was. What kind of maniac would be out on a night like this?

She sat there sipping tea and watching the hypnotic pattern the wind created in the whirling snow gusting over the lake surface. From the black curtain of trees came bright diamond spots of light. They moved swiftly down from the road to vanish behind the monolithic chalet on the other side of the lake. The lights glowed behind the house, creating an azure corona that described the planes and slopes of the rooftop. Her eye went to the cup of the telescope. A cloud of vapor, underlit by glowing headlamps, was visible rising from behind the big house. As she watched, a gloaming of light swept across the windows facing the lake. Someone was inside the house using a bright torchlight.

They were here.

Tonight was the night.

Lee moved to change her view from the telescope to the view screen of the Nikon. As she shifted her aspect, she could see a new movement below the house. In the green-tinted gaze of the night vision lens something moved with purpose over the dunes of snow covering the lake. It was cutting across the flow of the levitating frozen currents on an oblique angle away from the chalet over the lake surface.

Lee adjusted the focus to draw the figure closer. She lifted her eyes over the top of the camera then lowered them, seeking the moving object with her naked eye. She found the tiny shape and turned the dial on the lens to focus in on it.

The image of a girl leapt into view. A young girl, face pinched and whit,e with hair pulled back in a ponytail. She was struggling over a drift half her height, stabbing with her poles, lifting her legs high. She glided down the lee of the slope back to the flat surface of the ice. There she established her stride again and broke out across the frozen lake at a steady pace.

Unusual to see someone out in weather as wretched as this.

Still more unusual that the girl was dressed in a tartan plaid flannel robe over what appeared to be pajamas.

23

The world went black just as he fitted the last connection to the garbage disposal.

Levon Cade lay wedged on his back and blind in the cabinetry beneath the kitchen sink. He shut his eyes. He counted off to thirty before reopening them. Enough light came in off the French doors out to the deck to allow him to see his way around. He walked to the doors and looked out. Everything was dark around the lake. The pole lamps at the end of docks that were always on at night were out. The houses were invisible along the shoreline.

The sky beyond the trees was always dark because the nearest town of any size was away over the horizon hundreds of miles away. No light pollution in this part of Maine. Vacationland, the license plates proclaimed it. "Back of beyond" to the folks down in Bangor. No way to know how far this outage reached. Local or countywide.

He picked up the Hofferts' kitchen phone. Dead.

Nate Fenton was working on that water heater at the bungalow. It was electrical — the treacherous mix of voltage and water. Nate could be in trouble. At the very least, he'd need help getting the juice back online.

The new LED flashlight in his toolbox threw a beam of cold light that lanced through the gloom. Levon pulled on his coat and went out to the Ram. It started but took some goosing to break out of the frozen slush gripping the treads beneath the new snow. The truck leapt back from the ruts with a jerk. Levon pressed the pedal down steady and rose up to ride atop the snow, tires hissing.

An Alabama boy, he didn't have that much experience driving in deep snow. Sand was another matter. He had plenty of practice steering over sand. Same principle. Steady pace. Steer into skids. He pulled around the loop before the Hoffert house and down onto Mohawk.

Nate's snowmachine wasn't in the driveway of the bungalow when Levon pulled up. He sat in the warm cab of the Ram, wipers snicking back and forth. The nose of his truck was aimed at the driveway. Light from the big rack of lamps lit the drive and house front like a movie set. The snow at the foot of the drive was undisturbed. The tracks of Nate's arrival had been filled in by the snowfall of the past hour. Leaving the truck running but cutting the lights, Levon climbed out and walked toward the garage.

There were fresh tracks from where he'd last seen the snow machine and sled parked to the now closed garage door. The impressions were new, the pattern left by the treads and skis of the machine clearly defined. The house was dark — no light from inside. The garage doors had no windows to allow him to look inside. Levon tried the door handle at the foot of the fold-up. It was locked down from inside. Someone had pulled Nate's machine into the garage.

He crossed the driveway for the front door of the bungalow.

A droning hum rose from the roadway. A snow machine left the road to climb past the Ram, the skis leapt above the snow as the back treads dug in hard. Against the glow of blue exhaust, a figure clad in black hunched over the handlebars. The machine crashed down level; headlamps speared Levon, throwing his shadow high up the face of the bungalow. He moved out of the beam in a rolling leap. The snow rose in a neat row of geysers behind him. A string of sharp explosions rebounded off the surrounding trees. The muzzle flash of the gun in the machine rider's fist bloomed with crazed light that turned the world into a flickering monochrome.

Levon tumbled down the slope from the house, letting himself fall over a retaining wall away from the gunfire. He was in the dark now, back to the set-stone wall. A beam of light flashed through dark branches above him. The machine growled and rumbled as the beam swept past. He pushed himself off the wall and into the shadows between the pines before the light could return. The machine returned down to the roadway, purring along slow. The rider had a hand-held search lamp out now, playing it over the trees of the slope as he ground along at a crawl.

Levon stayed low, keeping tree boles between himself and the man on the machine. A big man in a black snow-suit with gray trim. He watched the man pull back the hood of his suit, exposing a head of severely cropped blond hair. The man stopped the machine and sat strad-dling it, playing the searchlight over the forested slope around the bungalow. A gleaming back shape lay across his knees; the stubby silhouette of a cut-down rifle of some kind.

It had been automatic fire that chased Levon out of the lamp's beam. Controlled three-round bursts. Someone who knew how to use the weapon. No hesitation. Someone who had killed before. Someone who expected to kill tonight. The man pulled a radio from the pocket of his suit and raised it to his ear and spoke. Levon couldn't hear the words over the rumble of the snow machine even though the man was shouting to be heard.

The radio was a little larger than a cellphone with a stunted antenna. Limited range. Whoever was on the other end was within a five-mile range. The other speaker was on the lake somewhere. Levon could hear the metallic squawk of the person on the other end. A male voice.

The snow machine rider was gesturing with the hand that held the lamp, agitated. The spear of light rose and fell up into the high branches. An argument.

Levon had a handgun locked in the glove compartment of the Ram, now thirty yards down the road to his left at the foot of the drive up on the high side of that retaining wall. A Colt revolver with six shots.

To his right, a good fifty feet away, the man stood astride the snow machine on the mantle of loose powder atop the ice slick surface. He spoke into the radio as he trained the light back and forth through the trees.

Merry was across the lake. A mile plus diagonal run to where the lake narrowed at the base of the neck of the gourd.

Levon rushed out of the trees and down to the road surface behind the snow machine, staying to the rider's blindside. He launched himself away, sliding between tree boles, slipping under branches bent low beneath burdens of wet snow. The rider's back was to him, involved in a heated conversation with someone on the other end. As he hit the level of the road, Levon broke into an open run, crossing the span in three long strides, knees high to clear the loose layer of freshly fallen snow.

Trees lined the drive that led down to the Christopher place. Big spruces formed a three-story double hedge at their base. He stayed among these, hugging the shadows, and listening to the purr of the machine on the road above growing fainter. The house lay ahead to his right, built into the slope of the hill. It appeared from the road to be a modest Cape Cod, roof dotted with sleepy dormers now covered with brows of white. The house opened up lakeside to become a three-story structure with a deck a half-acre in size leading down to a pool bookended by a four-bedroom guest house on one side and a boathouse with a sharply peaked rooftop on the other. Within was the forty-foot pleasure boat that was Tad Christopher's pride and joy. It was covered in thick plastic now, heat shrunk down on the superstructure like a second skin.

The lake lay open, flat, and leaden gray beyond a flight of wooden steps that led down to a hundred-foot wooden dock that ended at a gazebo. Levon loped down the gully of shadows between the structures for the top of the steps. Up on the roadway the snow machine let out a high growl as the engine revved. The headlamp played over the peak of the boathouse roof for an instant. The rider was turning back the way he'd come.

Levon reached the head of the steps while the engine above and behind him howled. The rider saw the fresh trail he'd left across the road. The steps below him were buried under snowfall making the wooden staircase look more like a slide. Without breaking stride Levon threw himself feet first down the flight, sliding toward the bottom, keeping his knees bent and feet up and clear of the stout wooden side rails going swiftly past his peripherals. His hands were palms down at his sides on the snow to control his speed and attitude. His gloves were back on the seat of the Ram. The cold stabbed at his hands as they skidded over the surface of the icy ramp.

The grind and whine of the snow machine grew louder above him. He tumbled clear of the foot the steps, letting his momentum carry him across a boardwalk. He slid across the slick surface to drop off the edge of the deck. He dropped six feet onto the hard surface of the lake itself. Snow drifted up against the pilings cushioned his fall. He paused in the lee of the walk and listened.

The snow machine was behind the house, clattering noisily over the big deck. He looked over the edge of the walk. Snow streamed down between the boards of the decking under the heavy passage of the machine and rider. The light of its headlamp illuminated the railings and hazed the falling snow before turning away. The steps showed no sign of his slide down them except for a shallow furrow. His back trail was undetectable. The rider would think he was still up on the upper level, perhaps hiding in one of the outbuildings.

Levon could wait until the rider got tired and left. Or until the rider radioed for more help. No idea how many there were. Or who they were. No point in thinking about that.

The light above turned away. The sound of the engine diminished as the rider trundled off the decking toward the back of the house.

Levon moved at a trot out onto the open expanse of ice and into the horizonless dark.

24

The three men appeared in the family room. The door off the deck banged open, startling Danni. The candles guttered and flared in the sudden cold draught. The men filled the room, looming into the pool of light from the camp lantern in the chandelier.

She moved to the children, scattering plates and cups and the articles of the board game in her rush to reach Giselle and Carl who stared at the invaders in mute confusion. A cry rose up from within her as she did so. A scream of fear, or roar of rage. It came from someplace primal. In an instant, without preamble or prescience, she knew these men meant them all harm.

Hands were on her, jerking her arms from where they reached to gather her children to her. Strong hands lifted her from her feet. A hand clamped over her mouth, filling her nose with a plastic smell. She kicked. She writhed. An arm pressed hard against her throat, cutting off the sound.

Giselle and Carl were hauled to their feet by a man in a slick black snowsuit. A fist wound tight in Giselle's hair, pulling her head back. A hand clutched Carl's upper arm, the boy wincing with the pain the grip brought. The camp lantern was sent swinging by the brief struggle. The glowing pendulum illuminated the face of the man holding the Fenton children. The light etched the shadows deep on his face before swinging away to return to darkness.

Even in the dark, the glow of one milky eye remained.

The man spoke to the other men. A foreign language spoken in a growling murmur. The tone of a man accustomed to being obeyed.

Danni was released. She fell to the floor, sucking air into her bruised throat. Through the roar of blood in her ears she heard the other men moving through the house. Banging doors. Boots on the hardwood. Hard voices.

Moira.

Where was Mitch's little girl?

She raised her head. The man holding her children was watching her. One half of his face was a mask; the dead eye and waxy skin were frozen in some kind of drooping parody of the opposite plane of his visage. She tried to speak. Her mind sought words, any words that might make this man release her boy and girl. The children breathed in gasps, shoulders rising and falling, eyes wide. Danni lowered her head, dropped her eyes from his gaze.

The other two men returned. A brief exchange. Questions from the man with the dead eye. Answers from the other men.

The man with the dead eye spoke into a radio. A voice came back atop an ambient hiss — a woman's voice speaking the same language as the men. The man spoke a final command and gestured to the other two with the radio.

Danni was lifted to her feet. She and the children

were led out through the front door of the cabin, along the porch and out onto the pathway to the drive. The swift bite of cold was a shock to her face. Something prodded her in the back. She stumbled forward, turning. One of the men held a shotgun. She hadn't noticed the guns before. She realized now that they were all armed. They were all dressed in identical black snowsuits. All wore latex gloves.

None of them were masked.

The man with the dead eye brushed past her, lighting the way with a flashlight. He walked off the drive down the slope to the roadway, following the narrow beam.

Her slippered feet were soon soaked, wool socks sodden with ice cold snow melt. Hot tears came to her eyes. She raised her head and swept her eyes across the dark line of trees on the other side of the driveway.

"No. No. No."

The man who prodded her with the shotgun pursed his lips and shook his head from side to side. A young man with a dark olive complexion and black eyes. He was almost pretty, with feminine features, but for a puckered scar drawn down from the corner of his mouth and across his chin.

Danni forced herself to study his eyes. She gestured to her children who came into her arms. Giselle and Carl leaned against her, hands gripping the cloth of her robe. She turned them and, arms about both, walked before the gunmen toward the roadway after the man with the dead eye, his flashlight casting a tunnel of light before them.

No Moira.

Where was she?

25

The opposite shore of the lake was still shrouded in the swirling field of windblown ice.

Levon moved at a steady jog, wary of his footing, keeping his center of mass balanced slightly forward. He paced himself, weighing options as he moved. With no landmarks on the featureless lake surface, he oriented himself with regular glances toward the Christopher house dark against the snowy slope of the shore behind him. He jogged roughly west/northwest toward the Fenton's.

Toward Merry.

Behind him, the engine noise of the snow machine rose and fell. He looked back to see the corona of the search lamp's glow moving behind the guesthouse. The rider still thought Levon was up there.

He trotted on, leaning into the wind that gusted over the lake surface. Stinging crystals of freezing snow pelted his face and pattered against the firehose canvas shell of his coat. He had no hat and no gloves. His hands were cramping. He flexed them, making fists and releasing them, to keep circulation going.

Before him, the haze of falling snow was illuminated by a sudden brush of bright light. Then a second beam crossed where the first still scorched on his retina. A shaft of light stabbed out from behind and above him. The racket of the snow machine soared to a rasping growl behind him. The blade of light lowered and lowered until it pierced the dark to his right in a jiggling beam. The beam narrowed and brightened. The engine noise was louder now, steadier. The rider was on the ice behind him, following that juddering lance of white radiance.

Three or four hundred yards back and closing. The light fell to the ice to his right. Levon veered away from it into the greater dark. He picked up his pace to a run. It was still a Hail Mary for the rider. He couldn't know his prey was on the ice. It was a guess. One man was like a grain of sand on the thousands of square acres of open lake surface. The snow and darkness would hide Levon unless the beam of light caught him as the distance between them closed.

His shadow was thrown long before him. His breath appeared in a blue cloud before his face. The edges of his vision turned incandescent with silvery light. He was trapped in the spotlight.

The snow machine revved with new urgency; a high pitched howl. The beam thrown against his back brightened and narrowed as the gap closed between the running man and the racing machine.

Something appeared in the gloom off to Levon's left. It glowed for a moment in the shimmering beam of light then vanished when the stream swept away to the right to train back on target.

An ice fishing shack. The two brothers Nate had told him about. He'd seen them a few days ago. Little specks out in the ice, visible from the windows of the Hoffert's kitchen. The shacks were roughly midway across the lake. That meant a half mile more to the far shore and cover. The snow machine would be on him in minutes.

The effective range of the rider's weapon was poor at best given the conditions. Firing from a moving base at a moving target in the dark took more luck than skill. The rider would need to close with him to improve the odds of a strike.

Levon hooked hard left out of the beam of brightening light and into the haven of the greater dark. He closed his eyes as he ran, restoring some of his night vision after the flash of the searchlight. The shack was fifty yards away. He broke into a sprint. The light beam washed over him, stabbing into the night to his left before swinging back to catch him full in its beam. The machine was closing in, near enough to hear the clatter of treads over the hard-packed ice. The rider revved higher, and the light beam slewed away sharply. The treads screamed on the slick surface before the machine regained purchase. The light trained his way again when Levon reached the shack and plunged around it into the shadow cast in the growing brilliance.

A simple eye bolt held the door secured. He slammed at the bolt with the heel of his hand until the frozen metal yielded. Levon leapt inside the shack.

————

The rider pulled up close to the shack and came to a stop. The glare of his headlamp showered onto the eight-foot square tar paper box. The rider climbed off the sputtering machine and raised the MP5 in his gloved fists and opened fire.

Starting at the floor line he peppered the shack with most of a magazine of 9mm rounds. Splinters flew as the lead punched holes in the walls through the plywood to come out the opposite wall. The single window shattered in a spray of glass. Empty shells clattered to the ice. He trained the weapon on the entrance of the shack and sent the last rounds in the mag through the door before kicking at it.

The door was hinged to open out. The rider's kick bounced it open off the frame. He shouldered it aside and poked his empty weapon within.

The shack was empty.

The running man was nowhere to be seen.

No blood.

The only evidence that the running man had been inside was a coat of firehose canvas discarded on a bench set on one wall. The rider leaned over to stare at the water sloshing in the hole in the ice at the center of the shack's floor. Black water with chunks of ice bobbing in the ripples left behind.

26

Merry reached the house to find her father's truck gone and the front door open. The wood frame around the lock was splintered.

Someone had been here.

Someone had forced their way in.

Someone could still be here.

She stayed in the tree line watching and listening. Nothing moved. No lights from the house.

Through the whistle and yaw of the wind in the trees, she could hear a whining sound coming off the lake. Like a chainsaw.

Or a snow machine.

The tracks of Daddy's truck were shallow furrows with the edges rounded by the snow. There were other tracks, sharply defined, recent, that crisscrossed around the house.

Her father wasn't here. He left before the men came looking for him.

And looking for her.

That was the story the tracks told her.

The power was out here. That meant the phone would be dead, too, just like at the Fenton's.

Hot tears sprang from her eyes only to freeze on her cheeks. She swallowed hard. She bit her lip until she tasted blood.

What would Daddy do? What would he want *her* to do?

Neither of them were where they were supposed to be. The men who came to the Fenton's seemed to know who would be there — *expected* them to be there. Knew about all about them.

But they hadn't known the Fenton's had a guest.

They came here, to the house where she and Daddy were living thinking they'd both be there.

Merry worked hard to sort it out, to decide what to do next. She tore her mind from the sounds she'd heard back at the Fenton's. Mrs. Fenton screaming. The rough voices of angry men.

What to do next? What were her choices?

Her father would not want her looking for him. Wherever he was, she prayed he was unhurt. She prayed in silence the way her mother had taught her. Not so much in words but in thoughts, trying to lay a blanket of comfort over the ice-cold dread grasping at her heart. She closed her eyes and prayed that the men at the Fenton's wouldn't harm them. She prayed for Giselle and Carl to be brave. She prayed that her own daddy was out there somewhere, doing what he could to stay alive. She prayed that he wouldn't worry about her. And lastly, she prayed for herself, for courage to do whatever came next.

"In Jesus's name, amen." She said this last in a whisper. That sealed the deal, as her mother used to promise her. End every prayer that way, and Jesus would hear you. Like a stamp on a letter, her mom would say.

Her heart rate had slowed while she prayed. Before it had been beating like it wanted out of her chest. Merry's breath came easier. The trembling in her hands and legs settled down. It was fear more than the cold that made her shake. She knew that.

Merry took a deep breath and let it out slowly in a fine stream of mist.

Two courses were open to her. Two ways to go.

She could hide, or she could go down to the county road at Bellevue for help.

Where would she hide? She couldn't go into the house. The men on the snow machines would be back. She couldn't stay outside all night. Not in this cold, dressed only in PJs and a robe.

With the help of the poles, she rose from the couch, her knees and hips protesting. She would keep moving. That was the best way to stay warm. Giselle told her that when she was learning to cross-country.

The market at Bellevue was ten miles down Mohawk Road. Cecile lived in an apartment behind the store. She had a CB radio in the store. They could call for help even if the phones were down there.

Ten miles. Merry had never skied that far before.

"So, I break my own record," she said to herself and pushed off down the gentle grade between the trees on an angle toward the roadway.

Merry stayed in the trees until she was well past where the road split to go around the lake. She was out of sight of any homes. The stretch of Mohawk Road out to the county road followed alongside a creek bed with curves here and there where it went around patches of old growth on slopes rising to the north side of the roadway.

There were no tracks in the snow covering the road surface. Nothing had been up or down this road in days.

It was an even and level course winding between the high drifts to the north and the gradual drop down to the creek bed to the south.

Merry set a pace that she thought she could manage for the long hike to the county road. The skis slid easily through the fresh layer of powder. Her arms pumped forward and back, forward and back, spiking the poles just enough to maintain balance and momentum. All about rhythm. Don't think too hard about it. Arms and legs pulling and sliding. The way Giselle had taught her.

The woods were silent except for the rattle of branches high above her each time the wind gusted. The only sounds were the whisper of her skis, the clank of the poles in her hands, the creak of the straps over her boots. Still, she kept her ears open to scan her surroundings. She listened for snow machine motors or voices. Nothing. The snow muted everything but her own sounds.

Ten miles. Maybe only nine now. Stay to the road and there was no way she could get lost. Concentrate on what was ahead not what was behind. She made her decision. She had to commit to it.

Daddy might go to the Fenton's looking for her. Or back to their house. He'd be worried. Maybe she should have stayed near the house. He could be there right now, searching for her. He wouldn't think to look down the road for her. The tracks of her skis didn't come near the house. She'd made sure to stay in the trees after crossing the road a ways from the house.

She was making good distance at her current pace, getting closer to the Bellevue Market with every slide of her skis. But she was still closer to the house behind her than the county road before her. She could turn back and be at the house, in her Daddy's arms, in minutes.

Or run into the men on the snow machines. They

might be waiting for her at the house. Or turning off the lake road to follow her.

Merry planted a pole hard in the packed snow and pivoted to a stop to look back the way she'd come. She listened hard but heard nothing but the movement of the boughs way above her head. She stared through the swirling mist of wind-driven flakes, looking for the headlamps of snow machines lighting the night. All she could see were her own tandem tracks leading back the way she'd come and disappearing into the moiré patterned fog of blowing snow.

The pattern was broken. Something moved there back on the roadway. She blinked hard. She wiped the crystals of ice from her lashes and focused on a shape growing from the gray dimness above the silvery pathway.

A figure on skis emerged out of the gloom. Head down, eyes on Merry's tracks. Poles lifting and legs marching forward.

Merry sucked in a lungful of icy air. She clamped her lips shut to cut off a cry. It could be someone else going for help. Her mind rejected that. Somehow, deep down, she knew this was one of *them*.

Leaning on the poles she turned herself back to the course and pushed off. She planted the poles, pushing and pulling, launching the skis over the hard pack. Breathing steady and even. Moving balanced for a curve in the road ahead. Maybe the person behind hadn't seen her. If she could make the curve she'd be out of sight for a stretch.

The follower was moving steady but not fast. They didn't have to. A grown-up had a longer stride. In a long race Merry would eventually be the loser even to an inexperienced cross-country skier. Merry had only been doing this a couple of weeks. Youth and luck were the only edge she had.

The road sloped down at a slight grade toward where the road bent to the left. Merry shoved hard, building speed, ending on a double push of the poles with all her weight behind them. She leaned forward from the waist and tucked the poles under her arms as momentum propelled her down the slope faster than her walking pace would carry her. Weight to one foot and then the other to maintain her balance. If she fell now, she'd lose some of the distance that separated her from her pursuer. Or worse, she'd hurt herself and not be able to continue.

Merry dug a pole in to correct her course away from the sharp drop to her right. She leaned to the left and slalomed around where the road cut into the hillside, the wall of a berm topped with tall pines. She looked back for an instant as the road carried her out of sight. The follower was still there, arms rising higher than before, moving faster toward the spot where the road turned down for the curve. Close enough now to see the blue snowsuit with double white stripes down the arms and legs. The head covered with a hood, the face with a dark mask that hid the wearer behind bug-like goggles.

They'd seen her.

On level ground again, Merry pushed hard on the poles to covet the slight increase in momentum the glide down the grade had gifted her. Her breath came in gasps. Her arms rose high, reaching out to stab points of the poles into the hard pack. Her thighs were ablaze with the effort. Her lungs raged with cold fire. All attempts at maintaining rhythm and form were forgotten. She could think only of escape.

As Merry fought her way down the frozen road, she could see her pursuer in her mind; a furious thing advancing with clockwork precision in her wake. A hooded, faceless creature that progressed with a sort of motion that she recognized in the way it moved its hips and set its feet. She saw the familiar in the silhouette that was pumping limbs to close with her.

It was a *woman* chasing her.

27

The water was blacker than the night above.

He struck out, legs kicking and arms pulling for the other shack.

The cold all around was not cold. It was pain. Hard, hammering pain setting his skin aflame. Knifing into his muscles.

Reach out and grab a handful of water. Pull it back and reach for another.

Training came back. Conditioning took over. The hours and days spent in ice-cold water at Dam Neck and Coronado came back to him.

The voices of instructors rang in his ears under the rhythm of his own pulse pounding in his ears.

Pain is in your mind! Cold is nothing! Water is just air, only thicker!

Dropped in freezing pools and ice-choked seas. Sometimes bound hand and foot. Sometimes naked. Sometimes weighed down with full gear. The shrieks of the instructors shouting from above reaching him through the fathoms of water. They called to him now from the past.

Pain is a bitch. Fuck that bitch! You tired? You want to quit? You want to die?

His muscles were clenched by cold fire. If he stopped, they'd seize. If they seized, then he'd sink. If that happened, Merry was alone. Grab a handful of water. Pull it back. Grab another.

Rising above the jabber in his head was one voice ringing clear and loud and true.

"You awake, Cade? Are you alive, Cade? Then move, you worthless motherfucker! You do not have my permission to rest! You do not have my approval to die! Swim, you weak-kneed motherfucker!"

Gunny Leffertz piping in.

Levon struck out with renewed purpose. Both hands stabbing out and coming back in a crawl. Angling upward for the ceiling of ice above him. Three feet thick in places. Like an inverted moonscape with hummocks and craters across its luminous surface. Trapped bubbles of air squiggled like mercury across the surface. Shimmering silver light filtered through the frozen upper limit of his world of suffering.

His throat was gripped as if by a fist. His body screamed for air. He tamped down the urgent animal desire to take a breath. Drove it down further and further. His total consciousness was focused on the swim ahead. His eyes scanned the ice above looking for sign of the shack somewhere on the lake surface over his head.

Lose it, miss it, pass it, turn away at the wrong angle and he'd die. He could only reach it on the first try. No second shots.

"Are you thinking, Cade? You are thinking, aren't you? You are using your imagination! That will get you dead, mother-fucker! Stop thinking about what might happen and kick,

damn you! If the worst happens, your dumb ass will never know it! The dead die ignorant! Swim, asshole, swim!"

Ahead of him, a smudge on the ice above. A muddy smear staining the dull glow cast from above.

He kicked and pulled upwards until he could touch the dimpled pack ice with his fingers. Eyes on the shape above that was clearly becoming the square shape of the second shack. Treading water, his hand found the bottom lip of the fishing hole cut in the ice by the Walbrooke brothers.

Levon kicked up and, using his body and one bent arm, wedged himself into the circular hole. The ice was two feet thick here. He shot a fist upward and struck a lid of ice above. Wriggling and fighting he managed to wedge his broad shoulders into the cavity. He twisted his neck and raised his chin to find a few inches of air trapped between the sloshing water and the cap of ice.

A sip of frigid air to fill his starving lungs. He ran his hands over the smooth surface of the frozen plug above. He pressed one palm against it. There was no room to bring both hands to bear. There was no give. He dropped back into the icy water for movement to room. He was free floating again in the shadow of the shack.

Regaining his equilibrium, he scissored his legs to shoot him upward. One fist extended above his head.

"One way out, Cade. One chance left for you and your little one. Don't fuck this up."

He kicked hard, eyes locked on the pearly circle in the gloom above.

———

The rider searched the ice for the spent brass. Crime scene discipline. Koning insisted on it. This crew was tight. Zero errors. Nothing left behind. That's how they all stayed out of a cell.

He was crouched, hopping like a toad. One glove in his teeth as he brushed fingers through the snow. His fingertips skittered over the ice, feeling for the empty shell casings. He counted as he picked them up and shoved them in a cargo pocket on his leg. When he reached thirty, he stood and snapped closed the flap over the cargo pocket.

He crunched over the ice to the second shack only because Koning would ask him. And the man would know if he was lying. That damned evil eye saw everything.

As he walked, he ejected the empty mag from the MP5 and stowed it in a pouch on the chest of his suit. He drew another one and secured it in place and drew back the bolt chambering the first round. Standing before the shack, he placed the weapon under one arm while he replaced the glove on his chilled hand.

He looked up at a sound just as the door of the shack exploded open. A white-faced man leapt toward the rider, a long gleaming steel hook held over his head. The look of a beast in his eyes.

28

"You understand that I must determine whether you are telling me the truth or not." The man with the dead white eye stood before Danni. She had to crane her neck back to look up at him.

They were in the family room of the lakeside mansion that sat below their cabin. A large room with furniture gathered against a wall and draped with sheets. A full bar dominated one wall. An entertainment center on the other. A huge walk-in fireplace of fieldstone rose up the bearing wall.

"I won't lie to you," Danni said.

Giselle and Carl were, like her, duct taped into kitchen chairs. Mother was set on the carpet across from her children.

"I must be certain," the man with the dead white eye said.

From elsewhere in the house, Danni could hear the sounds of men shouting. Glass broke. Wood splintered. They were looking for something.

"You understand?" the man with the dead white eye said. His voice was level. Flat. Even bored.

"I understand," Danni said.

"We are looking for a safe. A vault. A very special hiding place."

"I've never been in this house. I don't even know the names of the owners."

"Your husband maintains these properties. You help him, yes?"

"Yes. He does. I do help sometimes. But I've never been inside this house."

Another man appeared in a doorway. His snowsuit was off. His hair was white blond. He wore sideburns that connected to a brushy mustache like a hussar from back in the day. He was dressed in new mechanic's overalls. Latex gloves on his hands. Cloth covers on his boots. A sledgehammer with a long handle was in his fist. He spoke rapidly in a language Danni could not recognize. The man with the dead eye sighed and growled a command to him. The man in the doorway called back to others deeper in the house. It sounded like a different language. The man in the doorway was translating. He hefted the sledgehammer and retreated from the great room.

"We usually find the safe in the gymnasium. It is not there. You can see why we need your help." The man with the dead eye was crouching before her. His hand touched her knee. She recoiled as much as she could with the tape securing her tightly to the chair.

Danni looked over at her son and daughter. Carl's head hung low, eyes down. Steam rose from a puddle of urine at his feet. Giselle was wide-eyed, staring, searching into her mother's eyes with silent longing.

"Please," Danni said, turning her eyes to the stranger.

"Tell me where the safe is."

"I don't know. None of us know. We've never been in

this house. The owners haven't been here in years," she whispered, voice wet as her nose and eyes ran freely.

"You know. I believe you. I really do," the man with the dead eye said and stood.

"Thank you," Danni said, exhaling the air she felt she had been holding in her lungs since the men first appeared in her kitchen.

"As I said, however. I must be certain," the man said, his back to her as he opened a canvas tool case that rested on the counter of the bar.

"I'm not lying!" She was screaming now.

He turned to them, a pair of metal shears in his gloved hand.

"Let's confirm that, please," the man said.

29

The needlepoint of the gaff drove into the rider's skull with all the force Levon could bring to it.

The man's eyes opened wide. His hands went to Levon's arm. His only instinct was to remove the steel hook causing the unbearable agony spiking into his head just above his right eye. The MP5 dropped to the ice between them.

Levon fought against the man's double grip. He bore down harder on the rubber grip of the gaff, securing the steel hook in the bone. He punched the rider once, twice, in the throat. The blow was blunted by Levon's weakness and the thick fabric of the snowsuit latched tight around the man's neck.

Locked in struggle, the rider pressed Levon back toward the shack opening. The rider was a big man. Not young, but fit. Levon locked his knees, forcing the man to push back against dead weight. The fallen weapon was kicked forward to slide over the ice. The double grip on Levon's arm became feeble.

The look on the rider's face melted from fierce determination to dull fear. The grip failed as the feeling to his fingers fled. His knees buckled. He fell forward against Levon. The gaff was yanked from the wound leaving a furrow of ripped flesh and little blood. The rider was dead.

Levon fell to the ice under the sudden weight of the man. He rose to his knees and forked his arms under the rider's shoulders. He dragged the still figure into the shack. He straddled the corpse lying over the hole in the floor. Levon yanked the rope pull to secure the door. He set the block of wood in its cradle that held the door shut firm in the frame.

He dropped back on the bench, rubbing his hands together. They were drawing into claws against his will, the muscles and tendons seizing with the cold. His hands felt like useless clubs at the ends of his arms. His fingers were dead numb. Get those fingers working or die.

He allowed the waves of tremors that wracked him without resistance. That was his body fighting to restore circulation; his lizard brain fighting to restore his body temperature.

The blood returned to his hands. The rising pain was welcome. A sign that he'd have use of his fingers again soon.

His tremors continued. His system could only do so much on its own to bring his core temperature back to optimal. He needed a source of external heat. He needed out of his frozen clothes.

The Walbrookes had propane stoves set up in both cabins. He found fireplace matches but his fingers shook too much to keep one lit. The cock to open the propane feed took some effort to open. He turned it until he heard the hiss and smelled the rotten egg stink. Levon tore a Penthouse pet from where she was stapled to a wall. He lit a corner with three matches ignited simulta-neously. The slick paper caught. He waved it toward the stove. The gas caught in a brilliant flash that sent a dusting of black embers everywhere.

Levon stood and stripped down, leaving his boots for last. He used a razor-sharp gutting knife to cut off his flannel shirt, undershirt, pants and long underwear pants. As wet as his feet were, the wool socks were still holding in what heat was left.

Naked as the redhead on the scorched Penthouse fold-out, he crouched to hold his hands within the aura of warmed air rising from the stove. Not too close. Frozen flesh would cook rather than thaw. His fingers were soon infused with a pulsing agony as the small vessels opened to allow blood inside. Despite the pain and shivering, his hands would now obey him sufficiently for the work ahead. He pressed back against the bench and used his booted feet to lever the dead man onto his back.

The latches holding the breast of the snowsuit closed were the hardest. The zipper pulls beneath had nylon rope loops that he could hook a finger into. He stripped the man, dressing him down like a deer carcass. Now he could remove his own work boots and socks.

When he got to the man's two-piece Under Armour leggings and crew top, he pulled them off the corpse and onto himself. The cloth was still warm from the rider's remaining body heat. Levon rubbed his feet dry with a filthy towel he found on a hook. He warmed his feet near the stove until he could move his toes without pain. He then slipped his feet into the dead man's dry wool socks.

He reached through the pile of clothing lying on the floor by the body and pulled on the t-shirt and cable sweater and then the snowsuit. The boots went on last. All was a good fit, if a little roomy. The boots were too tight across the instep. He tossed them aside and put on his own work boots. They were damp inside. There was no time to wait for them to dry.

The short-range radio transmitter was in a Velcro pouch on the snowsuit's chest. A row of LEDs glowed amber across the top. He depressed the send button. There were two answering squelches from the speaker. Whoever was out there was maintaining radio discipline.

The radio went back in the pouch. The rider had nothing else on him. No currency, ID or any other sort of personal item. Levon's wallet and house keys went into pockets on the suit. He removed his Leatherman from his belt along with his buck knife and secured those away as well.

Levon searched the floor of the shack for the MP5. On hands and knees, he looked under the bench. He slid the body aside, turned it over. He undogged the door and opened it to scan the ice outside.

The weapon was gone. It could only have fallen through the hole in the ice when he dragged the rider's body inside.

Patting the many cargo pockets on the snowsuit revealed more magazines for the automatic but no other weapons beyond a clasp knife.

He stood a moment reviewing options.

The man lay face down. His back was inked with tattoos. They were good but not professional. Prison marks. A pair of dice reading seven on one shoulder. A fleur-de-lis on the other. The largest, a medieval lion icon, stood rampaging on his spine. They were all faded, the ink turned a blueish hue with edges blurred. The lion obscured a long-healed line of sutures. Not Russian. No minarets or crosses or eight-point stars.

Dropping to a crouch, he used the rider's clasp knife to make a deep 'Y' incision in the man's abdomen, from the join at the sternum to the mound at the crotch. The bloodless cut bisected a tattoo of a spider spread-legged over the stomach. The incision would allow any gases to escape as the body decomposed. The body would sink and stay down. He used his own belt to bind the corpse's ankles together. He tied the rider's boots tight around the ankles with the ends of the laces. Using strips of his own sliced clothing, he knotted the wrists together over a full case of Sebago beer empties, twenty-four bottles. The only thing of any weight in the shack. It would help the body sink and hold it down long enough for Ty Grant's trout to feed on face and fingers.

He tied a long strip of cloth around the body's torso and through the handles of the cardboard carry case before lowering the body headfirst into the hole in the floor. Levon lifted the feet to angle the corpse and drop it into the water. Water slapped the sides of the hole as the boots descended into the black water on the ends of the laces tied to the rider's ankles. A cascade of bubbles broke the surface; the case of beer bottles filling with water to further reduce the body's buoyancy.

Levon tossed the bloody gaff into the hole before exiting the shack and trotting to the snow machine that was still puttering on the ice by the first shack.

30

The vault was hidden under a cleverly placed hatch in the floor of the master bath.

The room looked like something out of a movie about the Caesars. Fluted columns and tiles from floor to a domed ceiling painted with a faux mosaic of water nymphs. Jan Smets found the hiding place using an ultraviolet lamp. It revealed some incongruous finger-prints around the edges of some of the tiles in the center of the floor between the Japanese soaking tub and walk-in shower.

"Time to go to work," Smets said and adjusted the tartan cap atop his receding hair, turning it around back-wards. The tap of a mallet shattered a few of the ceramic tiles, revealing a recessed ring pull beneath. He called for some of the others. They used a sledge to break the tiles all around. A five foot by three-foot hatch swung open on piano hinges, exposing the door of a stout steel vault door below.

A custom Mosler. The size of a coffin. Double bit key locks.

"Shit," Avi said under his breath.

"Thermal lance. Just enough to get inside the works. Make room while I get the tools," Smets said. He called for a man named Axel to help him.

Avi and Jussi took sledges to the soaking tub and threw the pieces into the walk-in shower. The water was turned off, so the pipes were dry when they snapped off. They were finishing when Smets returned with the magnesium rods. Axel carried the heavy fireproof gear folded in his arms.

Koning appeared in the broad arched doorway of the master bath. His one good eye swept the room. The side of his mouth that still worked twisted in a snarl at the sight of the dull steel face of the vault set in the recess.

"This will take hours. We don't have hours," Koning said.

"I burn a hole right here between the double locks. Then we see what breed of bitch this is," Smets said, drawing a rough oval in grease pencil between two brass keyholes set side by side in the façade of the otherwise featureless steel door.

"And if you like what you see?" Koning said.

"If the bitch is a whore, then she will open up for me without a fight. I have the tools to work the tumblers. A matter of moments." Smets shrugged.

"And the burn?"

"An hour to do it right, *chef*."

"And if the bitch is a nun with a cunt like the bank of England?" Avi asked with a scowl that reddened the scar tissue that ran from the corner of his mouth to his throat.

"We haul her out and take her through the ass." Smets wrinkled his nose and raised the cap to wipe away sweat on his sleeve.

All laughed but Koning.

"We'll need Visser. He has the muscle," he said and turned to go.

31

The earbud was alive with crosstalk that Levon couldn't understand.

The crew was Belgian.

The language was Flemish. He knew that much from the few words he could pick out. It was mixed with some phrases in Dutch depending on the speaker. He counted three distinct voices.

Questions came over the radio for someone named Visser. The voice asking the questions became more impatient when no reply came. Visser was unresponsive. He was missing. Visser was the man lying on the bottom of the lake.

Levon keyed the mike after each question for the missing man. Squelches on the other end would tell them that their man was still out there and having radio trouble. The questions stopped coming after a while. The crosstalk dissolved into occasional exchanges. Then the earbud went silent.

That meant the crew no longer needed their radios to communicate.

They were all in one place.

Levon gunned the snow machine and leaned low over the control bar. Snow stung his face. His field of vision was filled with flakes streaking toward his eyes like comets out of the black night. He could continue over the lake and roll right up on them. They had no reason to believe he wasn't their man Visser.

He had no real idea of their number. He wasn't armed. That plan wasn't going to work.

There was an M4 rifle with a thousand rounds of ammo locked in a gun safe back at his place. There was a Colt 1911 with four magazines secured under the seat of the Ram. Getting at either weapon would take him further from the Fenton house. He had no idea of the situation that lay ahead of him or what kind of threat Merry was under. Time was the primary factor here. He needed to be among the strangers with as much force, and in as little time, as he could manage.

He turned the snow machine hard right as he neared the opposite shore of the lake. All of the houses were dark, except for a nascent glow from within one building close to the water.

It was a sprawling house in a faux chalet style that was considered by everyone Levon met to be the ugliest home on Mohawk Road. It was the largest home on the lake. Danni Fenton called it "an architectural abortion." The Fenton's cabin was just behind it on the slope. There was much speculation about the owners. They hadn't visited the place in years. Or ever, as far as anyone knew. Their absence fueled rumors. They were drug dealers. The owner was a porno king. It was owned by a famous Hollywood couple and the home was trapped in divorce limbo.

Someone paid the property tax. Someone kept the home association membership up to date. And now armed strangers came to break in. It wasn't just a random burglary on a remote home. The crew shut down the electric and phone services. They spread out to lock down all the residents. And they had advance intelligence on who was living here. They needed time to do what they'd come to do. They established a secure area of operations just as a military unit would. They'd be here until daybreak at the very least.

The crew, some of them anyway, were former military. Their leader was a soldier for certain. That meant they'd act like a military unit. That meant Levon could predict some of their routine. He had an idea how they would react in most scenarios.

The snow machine clawed up a drift, sinking into the fresh snowfall until it found the solid ground that led up the slope to the roadway. Levon hooked a left onto Mohawk Road and drove straight for the Fenton's cabin. The crew in the big house would hear the engine roaring past. They'd think it was their man. That bought him time.

The earbud came to life again. They heard him pass. There were angry calls for Visser to answer them. He pulled the bud from his ear. The voices continued to call, tinny now, from the tiny speaker bobbing on his shoulder.

The Fenton's kitchen and family room showed signs of a violent struggle. Danni and the kids had fought being taken. Levon scanned the room, looking for blood traces and found none. It was abduction, not murder. For now.

In the master bedroom, he pulled the canvas case from the closet. He pulled the SKS rifle out and examined it. It was oiled and maintained. He slid the action back to open the bolt. The interior was shiny slick. The action moved easy without being loose. It would do.

On the floor of the closet was a plastic ammo box full

of stripper clips of ten 7.62 rounds. The bottleneck rounds were steel cased, but he could see no signs of corrosion. Levon shoved handfuls of clips into the pocket of the snowsuit. Three clips in either slit pocket on his torso. Four more in each cargo pocket on his legs. He fixed a clip in the top of the open action of the rifle and pushed it home with the heel of his hand. The bolt slammed tight with a clank. He drew it back again to plant a round in the chamber.

Somewhere in the house a door banged open. A floorboard complained under the tread of a boot.

"Visser? Wat doe je hier, lul? Koning is boos op je, Visser."

The voice was coming closer.

32

The road jinked right then left as it snaked between high banks topped with tall pines. It narrowed at the turns where the snow drifts piled high like dunes.

As she rounded each turn Merry looked back to see if the woman following her was in sight. The span of road behind was empty each time. The woman had fallen back for some reason.

Merry and her father had traveled this road more times than she could remember. In good weather they made at least two trips a week down to the market for one thing or another. She wished that she'd paid more attention to the drive. But it was only a ten minute or so ride from the market to their house. It was over so quick. Just another country two-lane.

She thought that the road straightened after the next curve for a long run down to the county road. As she skidded out of the concave turn, she saw that she was wrong. The road turned in a gradual bow on a downward slope into the shadowless dark. Merry dug in with the poles and pushed off to take advantage of the downhill run. Her shoulders burned now as well as her thighs.

The robe was getting heavier with snow melting into the wool. It made her arms feel like lead. She wanted to take the robe off. She knew that was wrong. Daddy told her once, when the weather got colder than she was ever used to down in Alabama, that wool will keep you warm even when it's wet.

"That's why sheep don't stand under trees when it rains like cows do," he told her.

She told him that was funny.

"Then you'll remember it. Gunny always says that if something is funny, you'll always remember it," Daddy said.

Daddy also told her once about the Wall of Pain. It was something athletes and soldiers faced. It was your body telling you to quit. Your brain telling you that you were pushing too hard. Your muscles screaming for you to stop. He told her that the wall wasn't really a wall. It was a gateway. And once you were through it the pain melted away and your muscles flooded with blood and your brain with a chemical that made you feel like it was your birthday and Christmas all in one. All you had to do was push for that gate to a world of euphoria on the other side.

Merry dug and pushed for the wall. She only hoped it came soon. She only hoped she reached it before the woman behind her could.

The gradual curve bottomed out into the long flat stretch of road she recalled. Maybe it was the knowledge that her goal was close, or maybe she passed through the gateway of pain, but her legs and arms felt lighter. Merry dropped into an easy rhythm, making good time through the trees that were sending sprays of mist down on her from branches whipped by the high gusts howling above.

Beyond enclosing ramparts of pine and elder ahead there, was a glow. A dawn light that grew in intensity as she pushed and pulled, pushed and pulled. It was the pole lights outside the market. As she poled along, the glow turned the branches and boles of the trees black before her.

Merry turned her head to look back the way she'd come. A tiny shape was visible against the white surface of the roadway. The woman was just coming off the apron of the curve onto the straight run. She had either fallen behind or Merry was the better on skis or, perhaps, the Wall of Pain was too much for her pursuer to get over.

Merry kicked a leg out at the end of the straight run and made the herringbone turn onto the broader span of the county road. Violent gusts tore down the north-south run of the road making snow devils over the washboard surface carved out by the wind.

The going was tougher here out of the cover of the trees. She bent into the squall, lifting her feet so the skis could clear the marching drifts. Merry leaned on the poles for support. The wind was racing down the county road like it was fed into a funnel and she was fighting her way up in the barrel. Icy pellets the size of BBs slapped her cheeks raw. She turned her face away.

Her pace slowed to a crawl. Head lowered, she looked up from under her brows. The pole lamps shuddered and waggled in the wind. Their twin glows were cast through the loops of hanging electrical wires throwing a quivering lace of shadows over the road.

Merry bent to undo the latches on the skis and pull her boots free. As she hoped and prayed, the snow on the road was a layer of soft powder over hard pack. She could make better time at an open run, hopping the high drifts. She was soon under the joined pools of light from the lamps dancing atop the swaying poles. Merry raced past the gas pump for the front door of the market. She turned as she did so to see a dark shape against the greater gloom out on the roadway.

The woman was moments from reaching her. She saw the shape seem to shrink. The woman was crouching, undoing her skis the way Merry had.

The sign hanging inside the thick glass of the doorway read: CLOSED UNTIL. Below the block letters was a picture of a clock. The hands were broken off.

Merry pounded on the glass and called out.

"Cecile! Cecile!"

She kicked the bottom door panel with her boots.

"Cecile! Let me in! Please!"

No sound, no lights from inside the dark store. Merry thought about running around the rear of the store. There was a door to Cecile's apartment back there. She turned her head. The woman was crossing the road toward her, stamping over the snow and into the shifting cones of light cast from the poles at the ends of the store lot.

Merry backed against the door. She held a ski pole in her hand like a spear. She wasn't at all sure of what she meant to do with it. All she knew was that she would not let this person lay a hand on her.

The woman stopped just past the gas pump. She reached up a mittened hand to pull the goggled mask from her face. The hood fell back with it, freeing a wild spray of ginger hair.

"Thank God I reached you!" Lily said, breathless with exertion. A smile of relief creased her face, now more red than her hair after the ordeal of the ten-mile race.

Merry lowered the ski pole, her own face crimson. Her stiffened muscles relaxed, and tears welled in her eyes once more.

33

Levon waited.

The bar of muted light coming in under the bedroom door was broken by a shadow on the other side.

His full weight was behind his shoulder when he struck the door, crashing it open. The combined force threw the man in the hallway hard against a wall.

Levon drove the rifle in his fists, stabbing forward. The extended bayonet pierced the man's forearm. The wicked triangular blade scraped bone on its way through the flesh and into the drywall, pinning the arm like a specimen.

The hand of the impaled arm went nerveless. The pistol fell from open fingers. Gobbets of blood were flung from the gloved fingertips.

The man's mouth opened in an exaggerated 'O.' A howl of pain and rage was welling up from his gut.

Levon drove an elbow into the man's temple, cutting the sound off before it could build.

"You speak English?" Levon said.

The man glared at him through red-rimmed eyes. A big man with dark hair pulled back into a ponytail. A dark goatee on his chin, a length of hair braided into a single bead of gold. On his neck, a tattoo of a Maltese cross wound in barbed wire. Professional ink. Not a prison tat like the man in the lake.

His eyes narrowed. The man was tensing to make a play.

"You speak English?" Levon said again, twisting the rifle to make the bayonet grind against the bone.

The man gasped and stiffened. The threat melted out of his eyes.

"You aren't worth shit to me unless we can talk," Levon said.

"English. A little." The voice was strangled with pain. Each word bitten off.

"How many men? What number of men are with you?" Levon's grip creaked on the wood of the rifle's stock, ready to make another quarter turn of the bayonet in the man's flesh.

"Eight. Eight, there are."

Seven now, by Levon's math.

"Where are they?"

"Big house. All at big house."

"Why?"

The man's eyes took on a lost look.

"Pourqua? Warum?" *Levon tried.*

"Beroven. Stelen. *To rob.*"

"Hostages? You have hostages."

The man nodded. He knew that word.

"How many?" Levon said.

"Three. Is three."

"Children? *Kindern?*"

"A boy and *een miesje.* Girl. A girl. And a woman. *De moeder.*" The mother. Danielle Fenton.

"How old is the girl? How many years?"

"*Tiener.* Teen. You know teen?"

Giselle. Levon's fists tightened their grip on the rifle.

"No other girl? A younger girl? *Kein jüngeres Mädchen?*" Levon's eyes bored into the other man's, looking for truth.

"*Neen.* No *jonger meisje.*" The man lowered his head and hissed the words between teeth clenched to hold down the growing torment from his stuck arm.

They didn't find Merry.

"I can't think of anything else to ask you," Levon said.

The man raised his face. Relief in his eyes turning to a feral glare.

Levon yanked the blade from the wall and the pinned limb. The man began a cry of pain that was cut off when Levon drove the bayonet deep into the man's throat. With a single jerking movement, Levon ripped the blade to one side and stepped away from the spray of arterial blood that erupted from the man's torn carotid. The bayonet was a stabbing weapon, not a cutting blade. The wound was a ragged mess. The man raised a palsied hand to stem the shower. He was dead before he could complete the futile gesture. He lay twitching in a wallow of his life's blood spreading over the floor.

Levon picked up the fallen pistol. A Sig Sauer. Extended magazine holding twenty rounds of 9mm. Another mag in the pouch pocket of the dead man's snowsuit. Levon wiped the blood from the pistol with a hand towel from the bathroom. He worked the slide to chamber a round. The gun was new. Probably purchased or stolen for this one job to be discarded afterwards. More confirmation that these were professionals.

And now there were six.

34

"It's going to be all right, baby. This will be over soon. We'll get you to a hospital," Danielle Fenton said like a mantra.

Carl sat mewling in his chair. His right hand was bundled in a bloody towel secured in place with duct tape. Blood gathered around the leg of the chair by his right foot. In the sticky mess lay his pinky and ring finger, severed at the base where they once joined his hand. Carl's skin was pale with shock. His eyes stared forward, dark-rimmed and running with tears.

Giselle was catatonic. She drew in breath through her mouth, jaw slack and eyes closed. She wanted nothing more than to hold her trapped hands over her ears. She wanted to vanish. Her mind fled from this place to someplace warm and dark and quiet. Her little brother's screams still echoed in her head.

"It's going to be all right, baby. This will be over soon. Just a little bit longer," Danni said again. Lies were the only comfort she could offer her children.

The men wore gloves on their hands and paper booties on their feet. They didn't smoke or eat or drink anything. They were taking every measure to be positive they left no evidence behind.

They wore no masks. Witnesses did not concern them because they were not going to leave anyone behind.

She was alone with her children now. The men were all away somewhere else in the house. She could hear their voices and the sounds of tools.

Danni pressed her eyes closed and prayed. She prayed for herself, and her children, and for Nate. She asked God to save them. And if He didn't have it in His plan to save them all, then could He save her children? And, if the worst was to happen, let the suffering be short, let it end quickly.

The prayers led to fantasy scenarios. Little Moira was able to escape and soon an army of state police would storm in to rescue them all. Or Nate would return to free them, and they would all escape together. Or maybe Moira's father, Mitch. Danni saw a strength in that man. His reticence to talk about himself or to brag. His easy masculinity hid a deep pain. Her sense of him was that he was a man whose anger, once roused, would be terrible.

She felt a chill gust of cold air wash over the room and opened her eyes. The sliding door that led to the outside deck was sliding open. A bundled figure entered the room ahead of a swirl of snow. A man. He closed the sliding door and removed a knit cap and scarf from around his head.

The artist. She'd only met him once briefly when she stopped by to introduce herself back in the fall. What was his name?

"Sascha?" she said in a hush.

He removed his fogged glasses to regard her.

"Help us. Get us away from here. There are men here who—"

"Stupid bitch," he said and turned to go deeper into the house to where the men were working with tools and fire to open the vault.

Danielle shrieked then. With rage. With fear. With the certain knowledge that her husband was dead and she and the children would follow.

35

Merry dropped the ski pole to the snow and started across the market lot to where Lily approached from the gas pump island.

Lily raised her arms. Merry thought it was to offer her shelter. Instead, Lily held one arm bent before her face. The other came up to point at Merry.

In that pointing hand was the ugly snout of a handgun. The bent arm was to protect Lily's face from the blowback of blood and bone fragments resulting from the point-blank fire to come. Behind her glasses, Lily's eyes loomed large and fiery.

A sudden puff of white down appeared on the front of Lily's snowsuit. A ragged hole was torn in the silken fabric over her right breast. Low thunder cracked, shattering the silence. The woman stumbled back, feet slipping, eyes growing wide. Lily fell hard on her back. She wriggled and flopped, trying to get purchase on the slick surface to rise again. Her gun hand wagged in the air, aiming at everything and nothing.

A second peal of thunder and Lily's head vanished in

a crimson bloom. Wisps of ginger hair joined feathery fragments of down whipping away on the wind.

Merry turned to see Cecile standing in the open door of store. A haze of gun smoke was shredding away on a gust. The old woman wore a white flannel nightgown over a red union suit. On her feet were carpet slippers and wool socks with tassels. In her hands was a double-barrel shotgun, the breech open and bleeding smoke. Cecile was feeding two fresh rounds into the barrels. Two spent rounds steamed on the hard pack snow at her feet.

"There any more of them?" Cecile said, snapping the barrels up and closed.

"Back at the lake. Men. They took the Fentons. I don't know where my daddy is," Merry said. It came out a quavering squeak from her constricted throat.

"Come inside, child. You're scared witless. I'll call Deke Bishop in Merton," Cecile said and held the door for Merry to hurry into the warm haven of the grocery market.

"Is he the police?"

"He drives a plow. The troopers will follow him down."

Merry was in the store and out of the cold but still shivering. Deep, painful tremors made her jaw hurt and eyesight jiggle.

"Never *did* like that bitch," the old woman said, casting a glance back at the still form even now being covered over with blowing snow.

36

Smets came into the master bedroom off the bath, pulling off a heavy Nomex hood and face mask. He was greasy with sweat and hurriedly stripped off the two-piece protective suit. Flecks of molten metal smoked where it was lodged in the fabric.

"Are you inside?" Avi asked from where he sat on the edge of the king-size bed.

"Give it a moment to clear. Jesus, I need a cigarette," Smets said coughing.

"After breathing in all this shit?" Avi said, waving a hand before his face.

Thick white smoke rolled from the bathroom. The cloud rose to the coffered ceiling of the master bedroom. There was a cloying chemical tang to it that burned the throat.

"No cigarettes," Avi reminded them with a wry smile. No smoking, no eating, no drinking. No trace of their DNA would be left behind. They even brought along plastic jugs to piss and spit in and bottles of chlorine bleach to splash over anywhere they might accidentally leave traces of any kind of effluvia.

Simon, known as Sascha to his neighbors, entered the room.

"You left the woman and children alone?" he said.

"We're waiting for the room to clear. I turned the fan on. It will take a moment," Smets said.

Simon snorted and charged into the bathroom. He picked up a sledgehammer as he did so. They could hear glass shattering within. An icy draft swirled through the haze, drawing it from the bedroom. Simon returned, hacking into his cupped hand. He dropped the sledge to the carpet.

"You are in a hurry?" Smets said with a smirk.

"You missed someone. A girl. She went for help or ran away or whatever. Vida went to follow her." Simon was agitated, thrumming with nervous energy.

"Where can a little girl go in this weather?" Avi shrugged.

"Visser and Loman were supposed to find everyone. We took care of the handyman. They should do their jobs. Where are they?" Simon said.

"Visser has radio problems. Loman went to find him," Koning said from the doorway. His good eye narrowed at Simon.

"It will be dawn in only a few hours," Simon said, voice quieter now, his hectoring tone muted in the presence of Koning.

"We will have the vault open soon. Go watch the woman and children," Koning said.

Simon left the room without further remark.

The remaining three men entered the master bath, the room still awash in a noxious fog. A stand lamp's beam was aimed down at the hole broken in the tile floor. Smoke swirled lazily where it crossed under the cone of light.

Smets took the tartan cap from his back pocket and

replaced it on his head before he dropped to the floor to examine the scorched front of the safe lying in the recess in the floor. He brushed ash and beads of melted steel away from the neat hole burned into the door at the center of the grease pencil oval he'd drawn earlier.

He snapped his fingers toward Avi, who rooted around in a canvas tool bag and came up with a scope with a flexible probe. He handed it to Smets, who clicked it on. An LED shone at the end of the probe with a diamond-bright light. Smets snaked the probe into the hole and fitted the rubber cup to his eye.

"How long?" Koning said, standing with a towel held to his mouth.

"Tenpins. I can see where the locks tie together. A coordinating mechanism with a flex bar. A shared tumbler with ten, no, twelve teeth. The box is custom, but I have seen this setup before," Smets said, drawing out a description of his view through the scope.

"How long?" Koning repeated.

"An hour at the most," Smets said, withdrawing the probe and sitting up.

"Call when you have it open." Koning left the room. He tossed the towel to the floor as he departed.

Twenty minutes later, Smets was beaming in the doorway of the master bedroom.

"I am a genius," he said without irony.

Koning rose from where he was lying flat on his back on the bed. He reminded Smets of a character from a horror movie as he raised his head then his torso from the designer duvet. The twisted face looked like a malevolent half-moon in the glow from the stand lamp in the bathroom.

The door of the safe stood open. Rubber wedges had been hammered in place to hold it so. The safe was fitted with steel boxes set in place to fill the interior side to side. They pulled the boxes out by the handles and carried them into the other room to dump them out on the bed.

Bundles of bills. Dollars, Euros, and pound sterling, all circulated and with signs of use. Bound in increments of twenty thousand of each currency. Clean cash. Two particularly heavy containers held plastic tubes filled with gold coins. Austrian Philharmonics. Hundreds of them. There were bearer bonds, boxes containing pearls, diamond bracelets, and earrings. A square leather case held neat rows of paper envelopes containing unmounted diamonds. Two carats minimum. Another steel box was filled with Rolex watches still in their presentation cases.

Smets and Avi shared a wild-eyed glance. This was the biggest trove they'd found yet in a Blanco house. This was the motherlode. It held the promise of the grand prize they sought.

Koning maintained his cold demeanor. He slapped their hands away from the growing pile of loot. A glare from his good eye made the two men back silently away.

Systematically, Koning sorted through the treasure atop the bed. He swept the cash and bonds aside to concentrate on smaller containers, envelopes, clamshell cases, and cloisonné cameo boxes that had tumbled from the boxes as they dumped them. He opened each, tossing aside gems, coins, mementoes, and letters. He examined each container until he was satisfied that it was bereft of the item he was seeking.

His hands brushed over a humble brown envelope. He undid the clasp and dropped the single item inside into his palm.

A plain black flash drive. Two inches long in its sleeve protector. Unmarked and unremarkable.

"Is that it?" Smets asked hoarsely.

Without answering, Koning grabbed up a padded case leaning by the bed. From the case he slid a seven-inch laptop and opened it atop a dresser standing against a wall. The other two men stepped closer, faces eager. Koning inserted the flash drive into a port and touched a few keys. The screen went white, and a dense column of letters and numbers appeared. Each was sixteen characters in length followed by abbreviated codes in capital letters. NCB. SNB. GCBA. VZB.

"That is it, yes? That is it?" Avi said, hunger plain in his voice.

"We are leaving now," Koning said and returned the flash drive back in its envelope and slid it into the padded case along with the laptop.

37

"We won't tell anyone anything. I swear we won't," Danielle said to the man she knew as Sascha.

He was seated at the bar, his back to her, absorbed with reading the labels of dust-coated bottles stacked on the shelves.

"They won't find us for days. You'll be long gone by then."

He sat unmoving.

"You don't need to do this." She whispered now, her words only for him. She didn't want the children to hear, to know.

He rose from the stool and walked to her. Danielle raised her face to speak to him once more. He struck with her an open slap, the latex stinging the flesh of her cheek. Her head rocked to one side, only to meet the back of his hand in a return blow that tore her upper lip. She tasted blood.

"There are no words that will save you," Simon said and turned from the sobbing woman to glare at the children who lowered their eyes, cowed by the threat of further punishment.

Through the glass doors behind the children, a man walked toward the house over the snow. Black snowsuit with the hood pulled up tight. A rifle slung over one shoulder. Visser or Loman. It was Loman, Simon decided.

Simon went to the door, unlatched it, and slid it open. The man in the snowsuit stepped to the open doorway.

"Where did you go? Where is Visser? Koning is angry with both of you."

A hand struck out, grabbing the front of Simon's sweater. Simon was jerked forward with enough force to whip his head back painfully. A fist struck him in the face three times in rapid succession. Three piston blows. One. Two. Three. His legs went out from under him. The grasping hand shoved now to send him tumbling back.

The man entered the house. Not Visser. Not Loman. A stranger. He held a bloody handgun in his fist. A spray of blood stained the sleeve and chest of the snowsuit.

Simon lay on the floor, vision spinning. Blood leaked from his ears and squirted in a thin arc from his ruined nose. The man stood over him and raised a boot over his face.

Danni Fenton watched in fascination as Mitch Roeder, her recent house guest, stomped again and again on Simon's head with the heavy boot. He stopped only after a heavy popping sound signaled that any more blows would be redundant.

Mitch opened a clasp knife and cut the tape that held Danni's wrists to the arm of the chair. Then he sawed at the bands holding her torso to the chair back.

"My God," was all she could manage. Tears sprang to her eyes as he pressed the handle of the knife into her hand.

"You can handle it from here?" he said, eyes level, searching her face, appraising her.

"Yes. Yes," she said, and bent to slice at the tape around her legs.

"Free your kids and get away from here. Find a place to hide until it's over."

"Yes. I will." Breathless. The tape came away from her legs.

"Where's Merry? Where's my little girl?"

"I don't know. They didn't take her." Danni left the chair in a shot and dropped to her knees before Carl to saw at his bonds.

"Take the fingers," Levon said.

Danni scooped up the little fingers from the pool of spilled blood and stuck them away in the pocket of her robe.

Giselle turned from watching her mother freeing her little brother to thank Mr. Roeder for coming for them. She opened her eyes wide, and a scream emerged.

Levon turned, dropping low. The SKS came into his hands in one fluid motion. Framed in the doorway was a man in mechanic's coveralls with a heavy leather tool bag in his hand and a tartan cap atop his head. The man threw himself back into the dark room as Levon opened fire, sending three rounds after him.

A crash of furniture and glass from the interior of the house.

A voice calling out. Another answering.

"Run," Levon called back to Danielle, and launched himself through the doorway.

Danni ripped away the last of the tape holding Giselle to the chair. She pulled both of her children with her out through the open sliding door and into the cold, cold night.

38

Deke Bishop thought it would be okay to get drunk.

He figured no one would be on the roads tonight with the snow still pissing down at two inches an hour. Nobody in their right mind anyhow. By morning he'd be hungover but sober enough to drive the plow. So he helped himself to another forty of cold Yuengling and fell asleep in a thick beer drunk in the recliner, watching a rerun of *River Monsters*.

The room was dark when Candy shook him awake.

"That was Cecile down at Bellevue," Candy was shouting. It set the dogs to barking.

"Suh-seel?" he said with a furry tongue. His head flopped forward when Candy tugged the chair lever to bring him upright with a sudden, nauseating jerk.

"Cecile Withers! They're in some kind of trouble! You have to clear the road for the troopers, Deke!" She stomped off in her galoshes, the dogs following, leaping and yipping.

"Shit, woman! I'm still shit-faced!" he said, leaning forward to put weight on his stocking feet, uncertain of whether or not he could stand without falling.

"That's why I'm going with you!" She stomped back in from the mudroom and threw his boots and coat at him.

Twenty minutes later, he was high up in the cab behind the wheel of the tractor pushing the massive steel spear point of ten-foot rollover plow south down the county road. Candy was strapped in beside him, pouring hot black coffee down him from a thermos. Snow blasted by in fifty-foot furrows off the twin blades that met in a ram set thirty feet in front of his grill. He gunned it as hard as he could, pegging the needle at sixty. Close behind, three state trooper cruisers and two county cars raced single file in his arctic wake, gliding along in the draft created by the big rig.

"What the hell kind of trouble are they in down in Bellevue?" he said, coffee roiling in his gut and sending a sour wash of reflux back up his throat.

"Terrorists. Home invaders. Something like that. Cecile said all hell's broke loose down there." Candy stared out the windshield down the tunnel of light the big overheads bored into the dark ahead.

"Cecile said that?" Deke said, taking his eyes from the road for a fraction.

"She did," Candy said. She poured another mug of cowboy coffee and held it out for his open gear hand.

Deke said nothing.

After another minute, he made a toodling sound with tongue and lips in imitation of a cavalry bugle.

39

Levon rolled to a stop against a Queen Anne curio cabinet that tottered on dainty legs. It collapsed backward, sending ceramic pieces crashing to the floor. The room was dark. The echoes of shattering china bounced off the ceiling high above him.

It was too dark to see any blood. He couldn't smell any through the oily reek of gunpowder. He'd missed the man in the tartan cap, only managed to drive him away. That worked for now.

The men in the house, four by his count, needed to focus on him. He had to be their biggest concern right now. The Fentons needed every second he could buy them.

The room lit up with muzzle flashes away to his right. He lay supine behind the fallen cabinet. He extended his arm above him and sprayed fire toward the flashes. The empty stripper clip flew away with the last round making a pronounced pronging noise. He rolled away from the cabinet to come against a leather sofa. A shower of upholstery batting dusted him as rounds punched through the chair back above him. Levon lay flat and swung the Sig Saur under the chair and fired a long volley.

He moved again. Up on his feet in a crouch, jamming a new clip into the open action of the rifle before skidding to his knees. No more fire. Boots on tile somewhere deeper in the house.

Levon stood and emptied the fresh clip in an arc in the direction of the echoing footfalls. Plaster flew from the walls in chunks either side of an archway. Powdered gypsum settled in the air.

He dropped the rifle onto its sling and charged through the door with the Sig in his fist again, held low and close to his body. He was in a wide foyer with a staircase rising along one wall. There were openings off the foyer into other rooms. The sounds before him stopped. The house was quiet enough to hear the snow driving against the windowpanes. He closed one eye, opened it. Closed the other, opened it. Restoring some level of night vision.

There was a source of light somewhere ahead refracting off walls, speckling the glass in the framed art prints that hung in a row down a long hallway. He moved down the center of the hall, feet sliding on the carpet to reduce noise. The hall ended in a cavernous bedroom suite. A bright glare coming in from an arched doorway threw the main room into a high contrast of shadow and light. An acrid chemical stink hung dense in the air.

Piled atop the bed was a bounty of cash and other valuables left behind by the thieves. He traversed the Sig from corner to corner, covering every hiding spot. The room was empty. He rushed to the opening to the bathroom, aiming the handgun at a sharp angle into the room. The stand lamp lit the room like a movie set. A wall of mirrors revealed the full range of the space within. The room was empty but for the mess of broken tile in the shower and the safe yawning open in the center of the floor.

Whatever they had come for was more valuable than the heap of loot they'd left behind, otherwise they'd have remained behind to defend it. Instead, they'd be making their exit with whatever it was they'd come here for. Back toward the rear exit on the lower level or out through the garage. He'd passed a row of snow machines on his way down to this house. They were pulled up on the apron before the open garage doors. Four total. Two had sleds hitched to them with steel equipment boxes open.

If they reached the machines they'd be gone into the woods. It would turn from a hunt to a chase.

It would be a chase then. He could afford to give them a few seconds lead. Levon turned back to the pile atop the bed.

40

An engine stammered to life, the noise rising to a steady roar.

Levon rushed to the windows along the wall of a landing. From there he could see a figure straddling a snow machine that was racing for the roadway. The rider was in mechanic's coveralls. Levon fired a string of snap shots through the glass. Gouts of snow marched after the machine as it rose to the flat road surface then out of sight on a straight course for the trees. The whine of the straining engine faded into the pines.

He remained on the landing in the stairwell that led down to the lower level. Below, the last three snow machines sat in a neat row on the turnaround. A rectangle of yellow light was projected on the snow from the open garage doors out of sight from his vantage point. No movement. No sound. By his count three men remained.

At the bottom of the final set of stairs was a paneled wooden door. Shut tight, but the bolts were shot open. Fresh impressions of boots on the carpet led to the door. The door would open into the garage; a big one with five bays. Two of them were occupied by cars covered with tarps. He pictured the remaining men waiting below behind cover. The rider who got away was the key figure. The crew's boss. The man with the loot. Whatever they'd found in the safe that was more valuable than a king-sized pile of cash, securities, and jewelry.

Levon retreated up the stairs, footfalls silent on the thick pile carpet. He returned with a leather upholstered chair he found at a rolltop desk in a study. The chair was wheeled. He pushed it into the stairwell. It tumbled down, rebounded off the wall at the landing and continued on down the turn to the bottom. It dropped from step to step toward the doorway to the garage. As the chair came to rest with a bang against the door it was greeted by the thunder of gunfire from inside the garage. The door frame splintered. Rounds punched through the solid wood door, blasting chunks of fill from the leather chair.

Ragged holes appeared in the walls at the bottom of the steps. Buckshot. Someone was in a space parallel to the bottom of the staircase. The chair was peppered with enough force to throw it against the opposite wall. A blizzard of plaster hung in the air.

Out of the line of fire against the oblique wall at the turn of the stairwell, Levon waited for the gunfire to die down before extending one hand around the corner and emptying the remainder of the Sig's clip down at the door and the wall. He dropped the handgun to the stairs and moved to the landing windows. A man in mechanic's coveralls raced stumbling into the yellow light cast from the open garage doors toward the row of snow machines.

Raising the rifle to his shoulder, Levon dropped him with three rounds aimed low to catch the runner in the legs and lower back. The man fell, flipping on his back onto the snow. A shotgun dropped from his fists. The man was clutching his side, hands clamped over an exit wound turning the snow beneath him pink. A tartan cap lay near him where it had flown from his head when he fell.

The wounded man called out a name in a croaking voice. It sounded like "Avi" to Levon. There was no answer from the garage. No shadow crossed the rectangle of light.

Levon shoulder slung the rifle and grabbed up the Sig and charged it with the last magazine from his pocket. He ran up the stairs and through to the great room for the sliding glass doors. The three chairs were empty now, hung with ribbons of tape. Sascha lay where Levon had left him, his head crushed into a crimson Rorschach.

Out on the deck, Levon followed the slipper prints through the snow and down a set of steps. He had the SKS to his shoulder, traversing the field of fire left to right over the triple path left by Danni and the kids that followed the wall of the house. She was leading them home. Like an animal panicked in the hunt and heading for the safety of its lair.

He dropped to the snow and followed the trail of the Fentons up the slope. At the corner of the wall, he stepped clear of the turn with the rifle raised.

Danni Fenton lay unmoving in the snow. Carl knelt by her, the bloody bundle of his right hand resting on her hip. Backing away from them was a young man in a coveralls. A man with Arab features. An Algerian maybe. A puckered scar on his chin. He had Giselle in a choke-hold, a handgun pressed into the curve of her neck.

"*Je pistool. Laat het nu,*" the man said. Eyes wide. Teeth clenched in a feral grin.

Levon stepped forward, rifle to his shoulder, the ring tang at the end of the barrel trained on the man's face.

"*Je pistool! Laat het!* The gun! *Nu!*" The man's voice rose an octave. Giselle stiffened as he jammed the gun tighter against her collar bone.

Levon continued his steady walk forward. The man high-stepped backward through a drift mounted against a wall of the house, dragging the petrified girl with him. He slipped. A knee began to go out from under him. He righted himself, yanking Giselle tighter to him.

"*Je pistol laat!* Motherfuck!" His eyes were wide, fixed on business end of the rifle.

Levon stalked closer. The barrel unwavering in his fists.

From the rear of the house the cries of the wounded man reached them.

The young man turned his head for a glance behind him.

Levon fired one round, taking the man high on the forehead. The man was flung backward, taking Giselle down with him into the drift. She screamed and kicked, fighting to free herself from the arm still grasping her.

Levon came at a rush, rifle trained on the man. Giselle freed herself and rolled away. Levon put three rounds into the man's chest. He stood over him. The top of the man's skull was blown off. He was dead from Levon's first shot.

Giselle was up and scrambled to her brother and mother. Levon backed toward them, rifle up, eyes searching for movement.

"Are there more men?" he said to the kids, as he swept the line of fire before him for targets.

"There was a guy with a plaid cap. And a guy with a messed up face," Carl said.

Three total. One of them on the fly. His count was off by one.

Levon turned to Danielle Fenton who was sitting up

with the help of her children. Strands of her hair were frozen stiff with black blood.

"What happened?"

"He hit her." Carl nodded toward the dead man. Giselle was hugging her mother, head buried in Danni's shoulder.

"Danielle? Can you hear me?" Levon said, an arm at her back to support her.

"My head hurts like hell."

"Are you nauseous? Do you feel like you're going to throw up?"

"No. Help me stand."

They pulled her upright, the kids supporting her either side. Levon gently pulled down the lid of one of her eyes with a thumb and examined it. The pupil dilation looked normal and focused.

"I'm going after the last one. Unless you want me to stay with you."

"The one with the white eye? Go. Go after him," Danni said in a weary voice.

"One of these men will have a radio on them. Keep trying it until you reach someone. Find a weapon for yourself. Arm yourself. And pack those fingers in snow." Levon turned and was away at a run.

Jan Smets had managed to turn on his belly to crawl for the closest snow machine. He was leaving a scarlet trail behind him on the snow.

Levon fired three rounds from the rifle into his head.

Levon chose the only remaining machine that was not hitched to a sled. The fuel gauge was at three-quarters full. They hadn't come far. Under ten kilometers. He mounted the snow machine and started the engine. It came to life with a sharp snarl. He was off in a blue cloud of exhaust, leaning from the saddle to follow the furrows left by the fleeing man.

One to go, by the count of the man he'd questioned at the Fenton house. One of the men could be a woman. The female half of the artist couple. Did she count as part of the team?

The one driving into the woods ahead of him was Levon's primary target.

41

The twin tracks ended where the snowmachine lay on its side in a gully four miles up the trail through the trees.

Levon slowed and stood with feet planted in the snow either side of his own machine. He trained the rifle down at the dead machine then to the surrounding woods to the north. There was clear sign visible where someone had climbed from the gully using hands and feet for purchase in the deep snow.

He sniffed the cold air. The tang of gasoline was rich in the gully. One of his shots had holed either the engine or gas tank. His quarry was on foot now.

Levon motored around the gully until he crossed fresh tracks in the snow. They continued north into the trees as far as he could see in the pre-dawn haze. He climbed from the machine and crouched by the tracks. The snow was tinged pink in the impressions made by a boot sole. Right boot. At least one round had found flesh.

The man was still moving at full stride. The left print was deeper. He was favoring that side. Blood loss or pain or both would slow him. He might just decide that an ambush was a better option than a dead run.

Levon cut the engine of the snow machine. He stood, eyes on the trees ahead. He took in a breath and held it to listen. No sound but the soft brush of one bough on another high over his head.

Wounded animals and wounded men moved downhill. They took the fastest route. The path of least resistance. These tracks led toward rising ground. His quarry wasn't running away from him.

This man was running toward something.

Levon double-timed, eyes on the tracks leading into the shadows of the pines.

The stride of the man grew shorter as the incline increased. There was more blood on the snow. The man's effort increased the blood loss. The left boot print deepened as the right grew shallower. The prints on the right turned eventually to a snaking trough. A leg wound. He was starting to drag that foot. There was blood on the bark of a tree where the man had reached out for support near the top of the ridge.

Levon came on the man on the downslope of the ridge. Levon had moved off the trail, making a wide curve away to the right and watching for chokepoints and possible ambush sites. He first spotted the man as a puff of vapor from behind the bole of an old growth spruce. Just a wisp of blue smoke against the gray.

He moved down and around on a buttonhook approach. Levon came upon the man seated with his back to the tree. The man's one good eye squinted at Levon through the trail of smoke rising from the cigarette clamped between his lips. One hand was clamped tight on his right thigh. The snow was soddened red beneath the leg. Levon's round had torn through the meat of the leg. An exit wound the size of a fist gleamed black midway between the hip and knee.

A handgun rested in his lap. With finger and thumb the man plucked it up by the end of the barrel and tossed it aside. His face clamped tight with the effort.

Levon moved up, the rifle raised, the barrel trained on that milky eye glaring sightlessly back at him. The man was speaking.

"A treasure. An obscene amount of treasure."

Levon was two paces away.

"And do you know what I thought of, all I could think of, as we pulled it from the vault?"

Levon said nothing.

"This cigarette." The man let a stream of cream-like smoke flow from between his teeth.

"Eight men. Your crew had eight men," Levon said.

"Seven and a woman." His skin had a waxy pallor all over now. His lips were turning white. He was bleeding out through the shot to the thigh.

"Lily."

"Was that the name she used?"

"You made it a long way with that leg."

"I could make it further. With your help."

"And why would I do that?" Levon said, no real curiosity in his voice.

"If I may?" the man said and reached his left hand up to tear open the Velcro strip on the pouch pocket at the front of his coveralls. Levon stood where he was, eye on the front sight of the rifle trained steady on the man's face.

The man removed a padded envelope. His glove smeared it with fresh blood.

"Do you know what this is? It is a simple flash drive. On it are the numbers for some very, very secret accounts at some very, very discrete banks all over the world."

"And I can have half if I help you get out of here in one piece?"

"Hundreds of millions in untraceable funds." The man smiled weakly with the half of his mouth that allowed for expression. His good eye glistened black now, the iris opening wide. The envelope dropped to his lap as his fingers lost their grip.

Levon watched the life drain away from the good eye. Until it was as fixed and unblinking as the milky orb set in the ruin of dead flesh drooping from his skull on the opposite side.

Levon drew close enough to kick at the man's right boot. Wouldn't be the first time he saw a dead man take a few others to the grave with a final surge of will born from fear or evil or both.

The man slumped sideways, limp and unmoving. His dead hand fell away from the wound. It was no longer bleeding.

Levon crouched by him. He plucked the envelope from where it had fallen to the snow. He shook it. Something shifted inside. He stuck it in the chest pouch of the snowsuit. He searched the other pockets of the coveralls and found a key ring with a car key and remote on it, a blood-smeared pack of Players, a gold lighter and two more magazines for the discarded Sig Sauer. He took the keys, lighter and the mags. He retrieved the tossed handgun from where it lay in the snow.

The cigarettes, the last desire of the dead man, Levon dropped atop the body before turning away to follow the hillside to the bottom.

———

Three miles down the long slope he came across a fire road cut through the woods decades before by one of the lumber companies. The passage of the snow machines the night before was still visible as parallel depressions in the snow that covered the road surface. He followed these back until he found a semi-tractor parked on the verge of the road. Snow was drifted up over the wheel wells. It had a long, empty flatbed trailer hitched to it.

Behind it was a pair of Suburbans with Toronto plates and strap chains fitted on the tires.

Levon tabbed the remote he'd taken off the man he'd left dead on the slope. Blinkers flashed front and back from one of the SUVs. He got in and started the engine and turned the heat up to full. Using a low branch cut from a pine, he brushed enough of the snow from the windows for minimum visibility. He rocked the SUV back and forth a few times until the wheels broke out of the snow. He pulled out onto the fire road, looped around and headed east for the intersection with the county road, chains slapping down the crust that had formed overnight atop the open snow.

42

An eight-foot berm of plowed snow blocked the county road at the south end of the intersection with Mohawk Road. The road north was plowed flat, the remaining snow churned by the passage of the police convoy that followed the plow in.

The sun was well over the horizon in a clear cloudless sky. Glare off the snow was already painful.

Levon pulled around the high berm along the shoulder, the tail of the Suburban swaying as the wheels fought for purchase in the snow piled on either side of the single plowed lane. He left the motor running on the lot of the Bellevue Market. A body lay in the snow, covered over with an Indian weave blanket. He pounded on the door which sprung open under his fist.

Merry was in his arms as though launched from inside. He buried his face in her hair, pulling her tight to him.

"The police followed the plow to the lake," Cecile said from the open doorway.

"How long ago?" Levon asked.

"Five minutes ago. Less maybe," Cecile said.

"We need to go," Levon said. Merry nodded.

"Might be best if you stayed here. They'll be back with questions. I have coffee on," Cecile said.

"We need to go," Levon repeated and guided Merry to the waiting SUV. She climbed over the driver's seat.

"They'll be blocking off the road," Cecile called after them.

"Thank you," Levon said and got behind the wheel.

Cecile watched the SUV leave the lot, turning south onto the unplowed stretch of road. It built speed, vanishing in the contrail of crystalline haze left in its wake.

She wondered if anyone would ever tell her what the hell was going on.

"I ran away," Merry said after a while.

"You did the right thing," Levon said to her.

"I left my skis behind."

"You're not going to need them where we're going."

They rode a while, not speaking, down the arrow straight white road. Levon pulled way off to the shoulder to allow a northbound plow to get by. The bighorn blared as it approached and blasted by. The angled plow cut a channel, leaving a miles-long drift along the roadside opposite of where Levon was parked. State and county police cars raced by after the plow as if pulled on a tether. An emergency response vehicle and several ambulances and unmarked cars followed a minute behind. Lights flashed and sirens yowled.

Levon didn't pull out until the road was empty. Ten miles down the road he came to a gas station at the edge of the town of Jedidiah, where he stopped long enough to top off the tank and pull the chains from the tires. He left them on the concrete island at the pumps.

A teenaged boy was at the counter when Levon went in to prepay for the gas.

"You see all those cops?"

"Passed them on the way here," Levon said. He poured himself a hot coffee. He pulled a couple of Snickers for Merry and a Payday for himself from the steel rack of candy. He added two bottled waters to the pile on the counter.

"You know where they were going?"

"North, right? I didn't pass any accidents or fires on the way here."

"Forty-eight fifty," the kid announced.

"You have a restroom?"

The boy pointed to a door in the back of the store.

In the tiny bathroom, Levon pulled thick wads of bills from the pockets of the snowsuit and set them on the edge of the sink until he had a stack eight inches in height. He found a banded pack with twenties in it and pulled a thousand dollars from it. Then he replaced the bundles in his pockets.

Back out in the store he put three twenties on the counter and waited for change.

"You been snow machining?" the counter boy said, pointing at his snowsuit.

"Yeah. I like to get out early," Levon said, heading for the door.

"Me too. Get out and make some noise." The teenager pumped his fist and grinned.

———

They made it to State Road 201 and turned east, following signs for Interstate 95. There were no roadblocks yet. Levon wanted to put as much distance as he was able between them and the lake community. The car was good for another few hours. At least until the evening when they could change rides.

"There's a Wendy's ahead." Levon nodded toward a sign along the verge of the four lane.

"Okay," Merry said without enthusiasm. She hadn't spoken since the gas station. She hadn't touched the candy bar or taken a sip of water.

"You have something you need to ask me, honey?"

"I'm afraid to." She played with the frayed end of the belt of her robe.

"Mrs. Fenton and the kids are okay. They're alive."

"And Mr. Fenton?"

"I don't know, honey. I didn't see him," Levon said.

"Those men. Who were they?"

"I don't know. Bad men. But they won't hurt anyone anymore. The police are there."

"Cecile shot Lily."

"That's who was under the blanket?"

"Yes. Lily was going to kill me. She had a gun." Merry's hands grew white where she gripped the belt of the robe.

Levon said nothing.

With a wet gulp, Merry broke into tears. She turned to him, her face stricken with pain, mouth twisted.

Levon pulled to the side of the road. He reached over for her, and she came into his arms, her face pressed into his shoulder. Her body heaved with sighs. He patted her hair and made wordless noises of comfort into her ear.

The Suburban rocked on its springs as car and truck traffic roared past.

43

Bill Marquez didn't need GPS to find the place.

There were two salt-crusted state cars parked on the lot of a pokey little gas station and market. Ribbons of yellow tape were strung from the pump island to the front of the store. Media was here as well — local and networks. Vans pulled along the road on either side. Dish towers extended from the rooftops. A few intrepid talking heads braved the cold to stand in the slush in the glare of camera lights to keep the public informed of what little they knew.

Another statie flagged him to a stop at the turn onto Mohawk. He showed his ID and was waved in. The trooper assured Bill that he'd radio ahead to let them know Special Agent William Marquez was on his way.

The road in and around the lake was plowed clean. There was yellow ribbon everywhere, marking homes as active crime scenes. State cars and trucks were parked in the drives before those homes. Hand printed signs were stuck in the snow before each home with the street address in block letters. He passed a big state CID trailer — one of their mobile crime labs.

The center ring of the circus was the Blanco house. Unmarked cars and trucks were on the road and in the drive. An RV was by the house with power lines run inside to share electrical service. Yellow tape created a maze around the house. Numbered markers were stuck on poles here and there in the snow, denoting places where evidence was located.

Bill carded himself into the Blanco house and accepted the paper booties and vinyl gloves offered to him. He was handed along by a trooper to a state CID guy and led up to the second floor where a forensic team had broken for a boxed lunch. From a balcony that over-looked the large center room of the open plan chalet, Bill could see three kitchen chairs draped with strands of duct tape. They sat two on one side and one on the other. The same scenario he'd seen before. A smear of blood stained the floor beneath one chair. Tape marked where a body lay. The area describing the head was circled by a dark mess of dried gore.

The forensics team was in the only room not framed in tape. A children's room decorated with posters and stuffed animals. The team looked like spacemen in their white Tyvek bunny suits, standing in a room decorated in a riot of colors.

"It's a fucking mess," Special Agent Ted Brompton said by way of greeting.

"It's the Blanco house, right? That's established?" Bill said, peering toward the entrance to the master bedroom. The bright glare of the high-wattage stand lamps glowed from within like the heart of a furnace.

"We found family pictures. Fingerprints confirm it. It's Blanco's house though he hasn't been here in a long time," Brompton said, picking onions off the tuna sand-wich in his hand.

"What did they get away with?"

"Better question is, why did they leave what they left? There's half my section's annual budget lying on the bed in there in cash. There's enough Rolexes for the office Christmas party. They either left it behind when they were interrupted or never planned to take it in the first place."

"They've been after a bigger prize all along. Maybe they got away with it," Bill suggested.

"Who the fuck knows?" Brompton shrugged.

Brompton reviewed the situation on the ground for Marquez. There were bodies everywhere. Civilians and otherwise. First impression was that the crew was out to eliminate any witnesses. There was a guy, a local handyman, found dead in a garage across the lake — two rounds to the back of the head. There was a retired couple four properties down from that scene. The man shot dead at the front door. The wife in the media room. And there were perps everywhere. Including one found in the woods about six miles north and a woman gunned down by the owner of the gas station down at the highway.

"Any early theories?" Bill asked. He'd reviewed the reports on the flight to Bangor. None of it made much linear sense. No clear timeline had been established yet.

"Thieves fall out? They found what they've been looking for and someone was reluctant to share?" Brompton said.

"Anything to back that up beyond pure blue sky?"

"We found that guy bled out in the woods. And there were two vehicles parked with that semi. One of them is gone." Brompton tossed a wedge of crust back into the box lunch.

"There's witnesses?" Bill asked.

"Three. But good luck getting much out of them,"

Brompton said, rooting in the box and coming up with a cellophane pack of cheese crackers.

44

"I'm sorry to bother you, Mrs. Fenton. I really am. But you know that I won't be the last to ask you questions about what you saw," Bill Marquez said. He was seated at the kitchen table. Mrs. Fenton sat huddled in a woolen robe across from him. She had not offered him anything but entry into her house. From somewhere in the home came the sound of loud pop music.

"I understand that," Danni said.

"How is your son?"

"They took him to Bangor on a helicopter. The doctors tell me they reattached his fingers. It's wait and see for now."

"You'll be traveling down to see him?" Bill nodded toward suitcases packed by the doorway.

"We'll be staying in Bangor while he recovers. Nate had family there. That's where we'll be holding the funeral. They're making all the arrangements."

"I see. I'm very sorry."

"What is it you want to ask me?" Danni sighed, lowering her eyes.

"How did you escape? Your statements are vague. You

and your children were securely bound. You told state CID and the Bureau that you were able to rip free from the duct tape. But the tape was cut by a blade."

Danni said nothing. She twirled her wedding ring on her finger with her thumb.

"I've been on this case, following this crew, for nearly a year, Mrs. Fenton. They don't leave witnesses. Never. They didn't let you go. So who did? Who cut you free?"

"Are you religious?" she said, looking up to meet his eyes.

"I'm Catholic. Lapsed."

"Me too. That teaching sticks. You may not go to mass, but you still pray, am I right? Every now and then?"

Bill nodded.

"I was helpless while my child was being maimed. I knew they'd kill my children and me. I knew my husband was dead. I knew we were in the hands of men with no souls. No mercy. I did the only thing I knew how. I prayed. I prayed to God, Jesus, and the Holy Virgin to save my babies. I prayed harder than I've ever prayed. I begged. I promised and I swore to dedicate my life to the Lord if only he could come and lift us away from the hands of those men."

Bill waited.

"And my prayers were answered." She locked on his gaze, defiant.

Bill pushed himself away from the table.

"Thank you, Mrs. Fenton," he said before letting himself out.

45

They were sharing a pizza in a Motel 6 in Waltham, Massachusetts.

Levon had stopped at a Walmart and picked up two changes of clothes in their sizes. A pair of sneakers for Merry along with a sweater and a winter coat. A fresh set of pajamas to replace the ruined pair she'd been wearing since the night before. Bags of socks and underwear. A gun cleaning kit. And toothbrushes, shampoo, and other necessaries.

Merry spread the new clothes on the bed. A towel turbaned on her freshly washed hair, snug in a new terrycloth robe that came to her ankles.

"And it's not even my new birthday yet," she said.

"Your birthday isn't until August," Levon said. He sat at the room's tiny desk, cleaning the Sig Sauer he'd picked up. Lying by his elbow were four magazines and two boxes of nine-millimeter ammo he'd found in the door pockets of the Suburban. He also had a new Keltec twelve-gauge shotgun and six boxes of buck that was in the cargo area of the SUV.

"My second birthday. Moira Roeder's birthday is in

February. The one on the papers." Merry smiled and took a nip from the end of a pepperoni slice.

"Two birthdays? Is that right? Well, you might be getting a third birthday."

"We need to change our name again?"

"Somewhere between here and Mississippi. I need new ID to get us a new car."

"Daddy?" she said, and took a seat on the corner of the bed nearest where he worked.

"Uh oh. That's your 'don't be mad at me' voice," he said, and turned smiling to her.

A returned smile grew and faded on her face. She lowered her eyes.

"I told Giselle Fenton my real name."

"What else did you tell her?"

"Nothing. Just to call me 'Merry' when we were alone."

"Maybe she thought it was a game, honey."

"Maybe. You think so?" Her face brightened.

"Either way, there's not much we can do about it," he said, still smiling.

Merry threw herself back on the bed covers to reach for the TV remote. She was pointing it at the TV when a gentle knock came from the door. Merry looked from her father to the door.

Levon covered the action of the Sig with his hand to mute the sound of it sliding closed, chambering a round. He moved to the door, standing to one side, away from the spyhole set in the center.

"Who's there?"

"Housekeeping. I brought extra towels."

Levon nodded to Merry who was off the bed in an instant and retreating to the bathroom.

Hand tight on the doorknob he spun it open as he rammed his shoulder against it. The door struck the person on the other side, sending them sprawling onto the sidewalk. The lot was dark and empty. He'd chosen a room facing away from the highway. A hand-held, small revolver. Levon stamped his boot heel on the wrist and tugged the .38 from the gloved hand. He dropped a knee to the visitor's abdomen, pinning them unmoving to the concrete. The hood of the anorak fell away, revealing a head of blonde hair.

The woman who called herself Leandra Tessler snarled up at him, eyes brimmed with fury. He tapped her chin once with his fist, bouncing the back of her head off the sidewalk and she was still.

———

"Kiera Anne Blanco-Reeves."

She came around at the sound of her own name.

The man she knew as Mitch was seated at the edge of the bed with her wallet open. The contents of her purse were spilled on the worn carpet. She was seated in the chair by the desk. She tried to open her mouth to speak but found her lips pressed together by tape. More tape secured her hands behind her. An electrical cord bound her legs to the legs of the chair.

"Are you a relative? A sister?" he said. He knew the name from the news reports already filling the 24-hour cycle with speculation.

She shook her head. A dull ache rose like a tide and turned into a ring tightening around her skull. Her eyes swam in her head.

"Don't throw up," he cautioned her with a sharp slap to her cheek.

A rushing sound. The shower was running in the bathroom.

"You're an ex-wife," he said.

Her eyes went cold. She huffed through her nostrils.

"Think you can tell me your story without hollering?"

She nodded.

He tore the tape off her mouth.

"That money's mine. And a lot more where that came from," she seethed, and nodded to neat stacks of bound hundreds visible in a bag by one leg of the bed.

"You knew they were coming. And you didn't say anything to anyone," Levon said.

"That bastard took off on me. We had a divorce settlement. Alimony. He ran out on all of that with that bitch of his."

"Stolen money."

"Yeah. He fucked some assholes out of their money. That was business. But fucking me out of my money was personal."

"And you just watched the house. Waiting for those men to come looking. And you were going to help yourself to whatever they left behind."

"That's right," she said with bitter assurance.

"Like a buzzard on a kill. Like a maggot." He tore a fresh length of tape from the roll.

She drew in breath for a reply to that. He slapped the new strip of tape over her mouth. Rocking in her chair, she screamed into the tape while he wound a three-foot band around her head to secure the gag in place. The sound started in her chest as a shriek but came out as a squeaky mewling. Levon keyed the TV remote. An infomercial for skin care products came on. He set the volume just high enough to mask the muted shrill she was making.

Levon went to the bathroom door and knocked. The shower water turned off with a squeak. The door opened and the little girl who called herself Moira stepped into the room. She was fully dressed in a new sweater and jeans. She slid her arms into a winter coat then walked past the bound woman, eyes averted. Merry picked up her backpack by the door and waited.

Levon zipped closed the bag with the money and carried it and the shotgun, wrapped in a bath towel, to the door.

"I'll call the office in the morning," he said before leaving. Then he switched off the room lights, leaving the room dark but for the flashing light of the TV making crazed shadows on the walls and ceiling.

Merry was walking toward the Suburban parked nose into the curb four rooms down. Levon tabbed a remote in his hand and another car, parked closer to the office, gave a short bleat and blinked its lights.

"We're taking the Mercedes, honey," he said.

"Doesn't look like any good news," Cecile said as she handed the bundle of mail over the counter.

"That's why I only collect it once a week," Danni said, and snapped the rubber band off the thick wad of envelopes.

"Still moving?"

"The HOA wants us out of the house. The kids are back at the cabin packing. Tourist season is coming. The summer residents will be showing up the end of the month."

Cecile made a *phuh* noise.

"They already hired a new handyman. His family shows up in two weeks," Danni continued.

"Where will you go?"

"Down to Bangor. My sister-in-law says we can live with her till we're back on our feet. I know what that means. Six weeks at the most before her husband starts giving us the stink eye." Danni riffled through the mail. Among the bills and final notices was an envelope addressed to "Danielle Fenton" in neat block letters. No return address.

"What will you do?" Cecile said. She poured a cup of coffee from her personal pot behind the counter and held it out for Danni.

"Thanks. I have applications in at a few daycare places. Maybe I can finish my degree. Try to get a teaching job." She tossed the bills into the trash bin by the counter.

"I'll miss you, Danielle. You're on my short list of people I can tolerate," Cecile said.

"I'll miss you too. I'll miss this place. But we can't stay here," Danni said and raised the coffee as a farewell.

She was behind the wheel of the car when she realized that she still had the handwritten envelope in her hand. She tore it open and found a single sheet of paper with a small silver key taped to it. The letter was written in the same neat block lettering as the envelope.

DANIELLE,
I AM SORRY TO HEAR ABOUT NATE. HE
WAS A GOOD MAN.
I KNOW THAT THINGS WILL BE TIGHT
WITH HIS LOSS. YOU HAVE TWO CHILDREN
TO SUPPORT AND CARL'S MEDICAL BILLS.
THIS KEY FITS THE LOCK ON THE BOTTOM
DRAWER OF MY CRAFTSMAN CHEST. IN
THE DRAWER IS A SMALL NOTEBOOK THAT
I WANT YOU TO BURN.
THE REST OF THE CONTENTS ARE YOURS.
THANK YOU FOR YOUR SILENCE.
BURN THIS LETTER WITH THE NOTEBOOK.
M.

On the way back from Bellevue, Danielle drove to the Hoffert house and let herself in. In the unfinished kitchen, she found Mitch's Craftsman chest; a wheeled steel cabinet with deep drawers. She knelt to place the key in the lock and open the bottom drawer. Atop a faded canvas tool bag lay a Moleskine notebook with a Bic pen secured in the spine. She put that aside and pulled out the canvas bag. It was packed full and heavy.

Inside were stacks of bills. Worn bills. Twenties and fifties bound in three-inch stacks secured with heavy rubber bands. There were dozens of stacks—close to two hundred thousand dollars once she'd finished counting them out on the kitchen table back at the cabin. She zipped the bag closed and secured it in the bottom of an apple box labeled "dishware." She taped the box closed.

Danni knelt before the stove in the fireplace, throwing pages torn from a book into the blaze.

TAKE A LOOK AT BOOK THREE:
LEVON'S RIDE

Levon Cade returns for book three in this relentless tale of action-packed retribution.

They could steal any car, anywhere, at any time. Too bad for them that they chose Levon's Ride.

Levon and his daughter, Merry, are on the run. When their SUV is stolen from a mall parking lot, it's up to Levon to find it. The car means nothing to him. But the million dollars in cash and uncut diamonds that are hidden in it mean freedom for Levon and his little girl.

As Levon sets out to recover his car and the valuables within it, he unintentionally discovers a widespread network of thieves and invites the wrath of a local gang.

Book three in the Levon Cade series offers more of the remorseless violence and high-speed action that readers have come to expect from Chuck Dixon.

AVAILABLE NOW

ABOUT THE AUTHOR

Born and raised in Philadelphia, Chuck Dixon worked a variety of jobs from driving an ice cream truck to working graveyard at a 7-11 before trying his hand as a writer. After a brief sojourn in children's books he turned to his childhood love of comic books. In his thirty years as a writer for Marvel, DC Comics and other publishers, Chuck built a reputation as a prolific and versatile freelancer working on a wide variety titles and genres from Conan the Barbarian to SpongeBob Square-Pants. His graphic novel adaptation of J.R.R. Tolkien's *The Hobbit* continues to be an international bestseller translated into fifty languages. He is the co-creator (with Graham Nolan) of the Batman villain Bane, the first enduring member added to the Dark Knight's rogue's gallery in forty years. He was also one of the seminal writers responsible for the continuing popularity of Marvel Comics' The Punisher.

After making his name in comics, Chuck moved to prose in 2011 and has since written over twenty novels, mostly in the action-thriller genre with a few side-trips to horror, hardboiled noir and western. The transition from the comics form to prose has been a life-altering event for him. As Chuck says, *"writing a comic is like getting on a roller coaster while writing a novel is more like a long car trip with a bunch of people you'll learn to hate."* His Levon Cade novels are currently in production as a television series from Sylvester Stallone's Balboa Productions. He currently lives in central Florida and, no, he does not miss the snow.

Printed in Great Britain
by Amazon